DEADLY SHADOW

The Assassin Chronicles - Book One

Kim Cresswell

KC Publishing

For Justin, Carla, Porter, and Peyton

In memory of Mary Beech
Death leaves a heartache no one can heal, love leaves a
memory no one can steal. — From a headstone in Ireland

ABOUT THE AUTHOR

Kim Cresswell resides in Ontario, Canada and is the award-winning author of the action-packed WHITNEY STEEL series.

Her romantic thriller, *Reflection* (A Whitney Steel Novel - Book One) has won numerous awards: RomCon®'s 2014 Readers' Crown Finalist (Romantic Suspense), InD'tale Magazine 2014 Rone Award Finalist (Suspense/ Thriller), UP Authors Fiction Challenge Winner, Silicon Valley's Romance Writers of America (RWA) "Gotcha!" Romantic Suspense Winner, and an Honorable Mention in Calgary's (RWA) The Writer's Voice Contest.

Kim signed a 3-book translation deal with Luzifer Verlag for the first three books in the Whitney Steel series: *Reflection, Retribution,* and *Resurrect.* The popular series will be published in German beginning in 2019.

The Assassin Chronicles TV series, based on Kim's upcoming 4-book paranormal/supernatural thriller series: *Deadly Shadow* (May 2018), *Invisible Truth, Assassin's Prophecy*, and *Vision of Fire* was in development with Council Tree Productions.

Web Site: www.kimcresswell.ca

Facebook: www.facebook.com/KimCresswellBooks

Twitter: http://twitter.com/kimcresswell

ALSO BY KIM CRESSWELL

Chameleon
Backwoods Murder

**True Crime Anthologies Published
by Grinning Man Press**
Serial Killer Quarterly "21st Century Psychos"
Serial Killer Quarterly "Partners in Pain"
Serial Killer Quarterly "Unsolved in North America"
Serial Killer Quarterly "Cruel Britannia"
Serial Killer Quarterly "They Almost Got Away"
Serial Killer Quarterly "Lostmord: Murder
in German"

PRAISE FOR DEADLY SHADOW

"A suspenseful, thrilling ride." — **Dima Zales**, *New York Times* **bestselling author**

"For as intriguing and raw as each page is, nothing, and I mean nothing, prepared me for that sledgehammer ending. Emotions will be electrically charged, feel the hatred, the terror and the determination of one woman to serve justice, one way or another."
— **Dianne, Tome Tender Book Blog**

"Cresswell builds sympathy for her heroine while simultaneously creeping readers out with her villains." — **Author M.K. Chester**

"An entertaining read." — **Amazon Review**

CHAPTER ONE

Within the hour, Derrick Lynn would kill his next target, a popular radio host known as 'Big Mouth' Bullington. He didn't want or need any specifics about the target, only who and when. He'd learned a long time ago to keep that distance to make his job a lot easier to deal with. Never women or children. Never a non-target—which at times took an incredible amount of self-control. More than anyone could imagine.

Like his grandfather and father, he could move about in real-time, watching people and events while his physical body remained asleep. The paranormal freaks called it etheric travel. But his real gift was psychokinesis, a gift very few in the world had. He used his mind to move objects. It came in damn handy, turning anything and everything into a deadly weapon.

For over twenty years he'd evaded the authorities —in particular, FBI Agent Victory McClane. And he was hell-bent on keeping it that way, no matter the cost.

In the large soundproof bedroom, Derrick laid on his back in his king-size bed, looking up at the ceiling with his hands clasped behind his head. Silk sheets covered his legs and, barely, his groin. The only light in the room came from the eerie glow radiating from the cell phone cradled in its charger on the nightstand next to his laptop. He glanced at the studio headshot of Eddie Bullington filling the phone's screen as the podcast of the man's radio show played at mid-volume.

"... and while it's a bunch of bull that Republicans work to keep the Black man down..."

His eyes shifted to the bathroom doorway to his dinner companion, Alessandra, a thirty-something runway model with long blonde hair and voguish features. She straightened her white blouse over her black skirt then put her hoop earrings back on. Alessandra shot him a soft smile and grabbed the silver faux-fur coat laying on the end of the bed. Before leaving she bent and kissed him, her lips warm against his. Derrick closed his eyes as Bullington's podcast droned on.

"... if you think the Dems are squeaky clean then I've got some prime Louisiana property for you. Those Limousine Liberals keep their boots pressed against the back of our necks, pretending to be on the side of equality and justice..."

He inhaled and exhaled slowly a dozen times and visualized his target's bedroom. His body felt light, floating. Before losing consciousness, he jerked himself awake, then let himself go under again. Deeper into a half-sleep state, he felt as if he were bobbing in a boat. As the rocking intensified, high-pitched ringing sounded in his ears and his limbs vibrated and buzzed like a bee's nest. He left the physical plane, his astral body flying.

❋　❋　❋

Eddie Bullington stood in the shower. Steaming hot water pulsated hard against the back of his shoulder blades. The "*God Bless America*" Muzak-like ringtone blasted from the phone sitting on the counter next to the double sink. He shut the water off, stepped out of the shower stall, and grabbed his regal-looking red and gold bathrobe from the back of the door. He quickly slipped it on and answered the call.

"Let me guess, Sid. You want to talk about last week's show."

"Sure do. Ratings are down five-percent from last quarter. That's a cause for concern."

"Just relax, okay? Anything else or are you going to keep on complaining about the same old thing?"

"Five-percent is a big deal, Eddie."

"Go to bed, Sid. I got this. I'll be in a little earlier than usual for the show." Eddie disconnected and shook his head.

His producer, Sid Moller, was a pain on a good day. Eddie didn't feel like dealing with the man's silliness. His ratings were fine. He was still the top radio host in the United States, his shows syndicated on four continents.

With the phone clutched in his hand, he strolled barefoot into the spacious antechamber located next to his bedroom and flopped down into the extra-wide recliner. After setting the phone on the end table he picked up the TV remote, along with a half bag of Cheetos. Eddie flicked on the TV to watch the latest episode of "*Tucker Carlson Tonight*" and dug into the snack bag.

❈   ❈   ❈

Derrick's eyelids fluttered. Blackness. Then a long,

dark tunnel emerged and grew wider. Sounds, natural and alien, came and went as a frantic rush of lights, faces, and places blazed toward him. He bobbed and weaved. Images, some distinct, others not, warped and flew toward him, through him, past him. The sounds and images intensified. Then they stopped. He was in Bullington's bedroom.

*　　*　　*

Derrick stood behind Eddie, his naked body blurry and silhouetted in shadow. The room was filled with over-stuffed antique furniture, gaudy gold and green patterned drapes, and a Victorian rug in various hideous shades of red and pink. A mounted rhinoceros head glared down at it all.

His eyes shifted to the end table, then to Eddie's phone. He trembled. Sweat dripped from his forehead and ran down the sides of his face. His gaze moved to the colorful ad for gold on the TV screen while the male announcer excitedly implored viewers to act now because there has never been a better time to buy. Derrick directed his energy at the end table drawer. It quietly eased open. Inside was a Baby Glock. He concentrated harder, staring, focusing as much energy as he could at the weapon.

The gun twitched. And turned. And rose from the drawer. The barrel moved within an inch from Bullington's right temple.

Eddie twisted his head as if sensing something was about to happen. "What the—"

An angry gunshot cracked.

Blood, bone, and brain matter splattered and

sprayed across the room. Various colored fluids and small lumps ran down the TV from a splotch at the top of the screen.

Derrick grunted. The gun traveled back to the end table and the drawer slammed shut.

* * *

Derrick's physical body and astral body snapped together like strong magnets, slamming him back into the bed. His body jerked. Intermittent banging and dinging invaded his head. Then the familiar headache kicked in. Like an elastic band tight around his forehead, traveling down the base of his skull. His eyes jolted open. He stared for a long moment, disoriented, before slowly sitting up in bed. Bullington's podcast continued to play.

"... oh, yeah. Give them freedom then lock them up in prison cages for years. That's all I'm saying. Thanks for tuning in."

Once he got his bearings, Derrick grabbed his laptop from the nightstand and opened the lid. The brilliant screen illuminated his tense face as it booted up.

He opened a new email and typed 'task completed', encrypted the data, then tapped the 'send' button. It would only be a matter of seconds before he received confirmation that the payment had been transferred to his account at the Panama National Bank under the name, Miles McGrath. A million dollars. Not bad for less than two hours work including surveillance. A soft beep. Then a message popped up on the screen.

((0400TCHCLVGHEPUOFJJHPLJO7IAJKHBG2NDLF))

With a couple of keystrokes, he ran the special decryption software he'd been given, and within seconds the garbled message became readable.

Fee transferred. Face-to-face requested

He shut down the laptop and wondered why his contact had requested a meeting in person. His face reflected on the black screen, yet his blue eyes shone.

CHAPTER TWO

In the warmth of the SUV, Victory clutched her cup of coffee with both hands and stared at her partner.

Ryan glanced at her, then back to the road. "I'm still thinking."

"You've been thinking for five minutes, at least."

"Okay." He sighed. "His father is...my father's son...and I have no siblings."

"That's established."

"My father's son...me...is...my grandfather. The man is my grandfather." He slapped the steering wheel in triumph, then flicked on the turning signal and turned right.

"How'd you ever become an FBI agent?"

"My uncle bought my way in." He grinned. "Is it his uncle?"

"What?"

"That man's father is his uncle."

"No. Jesus C—"

The car ahead came to a dead stop.

"Watch out, Ryan!"

"Jesus." He stomped the brake.

The seatbelt tightened across her chest. Luke-warm coffee splashed onto her jeans. The Chevy Suburban fish-tailed and slid on the snow-covered road, finally coming to a stop almost kissing the bumper of the car ahead. The driver of the car suddenly turned on his hazard lights.

Ryan tossed the vehicle into reverse, and then drove around the car.

Victory set her coffee in the holder between the seats and glared at the driver as they passed. "A little late for that, don't ya think, pal?"

The driver gave her the finger.

She shook her head. "Moron. Don't people stay home anymore in crappy weather?"

"Guess not. The first November snowfall brings out all the idiots."

She hated November. Hated the snow. It reminded her of death.

"You seem a little off tonight, Vic. You okay?"

"Eighteen-hour day so far and no end in sight, apparently. I hate celebrity crimes. And I'm going to be forty-five years old in a couple days. That's halfway to fifty, in case your math skills are as poor as your riddle-solving skills. At least Jade's coming home for my birthday so there's that but, Jesus...forty-five."

"I can't imagine."

"Says the guy born nine days after me."

"Hey, I'm just a kid compared to you, and always will be."

Victory watched the giant snowflakes disintegrate on the windshield. "Man, what do you think we'll find there? The friggin' ghost of Houdini? I doubt it's nearly as perplexing as we've been told. We shouldn't have to deal with this, not when...why aren't the locals handling it?"

"Bullington was an important guy."

"He wasn't the least bit important."

"He was hugely popular." Popular and important have become synonyms in this wacky new age of alternate facts and the divine right of media personalities," Ryan said dismissively before returning to the issue at hand. "I guess when the Bureau was called in, the brass figured they needed the top players for this game."

"Like the guy who can't figure out a simple riddle and his elderly partner?"

"Is it my cousin?"

Victory shook her head again. "You ever listen to him? Bullington?"

"Hardly my cup of Sanka. I'm not big on politics or government conspiracies. Except for JFK. That one still doesn't feel right to me."

"Someone told me Bullington said the Obama birther thing was just a ruse to obfuscate the fact he really came from..." She pointed out the window at the sky. "...up there somewhere and dropped in to find out what really happened to his pals at Area 51 back in the day."

"Well, the Bullington-types always said he was some kind of alien."

Victory rolled her eyes.

Ryan grinned. "So Big Mouth was kooky, or just capitalized well off other kooks, but I don't know who would've wanted to blow his brains out."

The guy hadn't earned the name 'Big Mouth' for keeping his big mouth shut. He was controversial about anything and everything from gun control to religion to racism. There was probably a mile-long list of people who wanted to shut the man up for good.

Victory took a drink of her coffee. "Profiting from others, further dividing the country and fueling dissent for no reason other than money and fame? Who wouldn't want to kill him?"

"Point taken," Ryan said.

Flashing red and blue lights came into view ahead, and so did Eddie Bullington's vulgar gated mansion, lit to the hilt.

Ryan stopped the SUV behind one of the many police cruisers parked on the street.

Victory pulled the FBI badge that was hanging down her shirt and put it on the outside of her Bureau-issued winter coat. They opened their doors at the same time and got out of the vehicle.

*   *   *

In the enormous foyer of Bullington's home in the affluent North Avondale neighborhood, Victory and Ryan put on a pair of Nitrile gloves and protective booties.

She stopped a young rookie officer heading toward the front door. "Who's the lead?"

"That'd be Detective Lynch. He's up there." He nodded to the stairs. "He's the guy in the Cardinals ball cap."

"Thanks." She and Ryan climbed the grand winding staircase that seemed to go on forever. At the top, to the right, they entered a massive room, an antechamber, connected to the man's bedroom.

"Christ, Vic. Your whole apartment could fit in here. Be a swell place to live, huh?"

Ryan was right about the room's pointless immensity. To fill space, it was embellished in what she could only describe as Victorian ugly. Red, gold, floral, ornate. Not her taste, that's for sure. She preferred modern contemporary, and simple, functional.

Victory glanced at the rhinoceros head mounted on the wall and frowned. "It wouldn't be so swell if I had to take this hideous decadence as part of the deal. I couldn't."

After they exchanged a few quick pleasantries with a couple of local cops they knew, Victory found Detective Lynch. He was tall and slim, wearing an over-sized black T-shirt and faded jeans. His gold shield was clipped to his leather belt next to his weapon and cell phone.

"Detective Lynch, I'm Victory McClane. This is my partner, Ryan Slater."

Lynch nodded. "Good to meet you both. Just got off the phone with the M.E. It'll be another half-hour or so before he gets here." He ran his fingers through his short-cropped hair. "You know, I've been doing this gig for a lot of years. Never seen anything as perplexing. Not entirely sure why you guys got called in, though."

"Early speculation about domestic terrorism. NSM, that sort of thing," Ryan said.

"The National Socialists? Yeah, crossed my mind. Or any radical group, really. The guy offended just about everybody. A genuine equal opportunity offender."

Victory scanned the scene to see if anything stood out. The room was obsessively neat and clean, other than the dead guy in the chair. A single shell casing was on the rug, tagged with an evidence marker.

"Who found him?" Ryan asked.

"Couple of our locals. One of his producers called it in. Said Bullington was a no-show for his radio show. The producer called him and didn't get an answer, which was apparently unheard of too. Our guys did a welfare check, busted in, and this is the mess we ended up with."

Victory's attention traveled to the large African-American male with a quarter-size hole through his right temple. A chunk of his skull was gone. The flesh around his eyes was bluish-black and swollen shut. She noted the gunpowder burn surrounding the bullet's entry point. Shot at close range. One hand was holding a bag of Cheetos. The other hand was inside the bag.

"Obviously, nothing's been moved since your guys arrived," she said.

"Just the gun, dusted for prints. The media's gonna get hard over this so we're acutely aware that no screw-ups can taint the investigation."

Victory and Ryan peered inside the snack bag at Bullington's hand still clenching a handful of Cheetos.

"We look bad enough already with The Wrapper still not apprehended. People aren't too keen about a serial killer roaming the streets. We sure don't need to be adding insult to injury. Guess you guys are on the same carnival ride?"

Now the detective was annoying her. Victory stood ram-rod straight. Ryan stepped in before she had the chance to say something confrontational.

"It's more common to finish your snack before doing yourself like that."

"Sloppiest staged suicide I ever saw." Lynch shook his head. Yet...not a single damn sign so far of anyone being in here but him."

"No maids, cleaners with access?" Ryan asked.

Lynch shook his head again. "None on duty, and none with keys as far as we've been able to find out so far. All employees are being checked out."

Victory looked at the Glock in the open drawer of the end table. "Gun been fired recently?"

"Yup. And no prints but his own. The weapon's legit, too," Lynch said. "Registered to Bullington. He was apparently shaken by death threats from the National Socialist Movement. Can't blame him. They're as crazy as he was."

Victory was aware of the neo-Nazi group, the largest and most active group in the country. She had heard the FBI had launched a hate crime investigation into the NSM immediately after the threats against Bullington. Had the NSM made good on their threat?

Ryan looked at Lynch. "Anyone from the NSM been contacted yet?"

"Still working on it. Nobody answers their phone in the middle of the night anymore, ringers are off—well except for us. You haven't seen the weirdest part yet. Come with me."

They followed the detective into the hallway.

"Our guy had one hell of a security setup. This is just the secondary system." Lynch headed to the stair railing and yelled downstairs. "Hey, Tomlin!"

"Yo."

"Make that call again, will ya."

"Sure."

Lynch rejoined them. "Step back into that doorway for a moment, would ya?"

Victory glanced at Ryan. He shrugged, unsure what to expect either. They moved back into the antechamber doorway and waited. Lynch stepped into the doorway across from them.

A few moments passed, then the lights in the hallway turned off. Red dual-beam lasers crisscrossed the length and width of the hall and reflected off the glistening black marble floor.

Ryan's eyes widened. "Now there's something different."

"Bet you haven't seen anything like this in a private residence. I sure as hell haven't," Lynch said.

"Guess he took the threats seriously. How ironic that the best security system hadn't kept the man safe," Ryan said.

"That's not actually irony," Victory pointed out.

"What? Sure it—"

Lynch cut in. "You're going to want to cover your ears now."

Victory's eyebrows rose.

He swiped his hand through the lasers and tripped the ear-splitting alarm. Victory and Ryan quickly covered their ears. A few beats passed, and the alarm shut off and the lasers disappeared.

Lynch leaned against the doorframe. "Security company's logs show Bullington arrived home at four-forty-three pm. He reset the main alarm at that time and called to activate the secondary at seven-fifteen."

"Can they verify it was Bullington who called?" Ryan asked.

The hairs on the back of Victory's neck prickled. A whispery sound filled her ears, like light wind through brittle leaves. Something touched her face. She raised her hand to her cheek but there was nothing there. Her gaze darted between Ryan and Lynch. They were oblivious to what she had experienced. *McClane, keep it together. You're just tired.*

"It could have been the killer," Ryan said.

"What?" Victory tried not to sound alarmed.

"Computerized voice-print technology. The system won't activate if it's not Bullington," Lynch explained.

Victory's hands turned clammy. She was still shaken by what she had experienced. She stripped off the gloves and stuffed them in her coat pocket. "Windows? Doors?"

Lynch shook his head. "No forced entry. Locked and barred."

"Has his next-of-kin been contacted?" Victory asked.

"Not yet."

She didn't want the media to find out before the victim's family had been notified. "Okay, we'll take over from here. Thanks for all your help."

"You bet. And you're more than welcome to this one. Consider this your official invite." Detective Lynch scratched his head. "But tell me—how the hell did the perp get in and out of a house locked up tighter than Fort Knox?"

CHAPTER THREE

The faint light emanating from the rusty and dented light fixture precariously dangling from the ceiling, cast a dusty halo against the warehouse floor. The man zipped up the white Haz-Mat-type protective suit, then bent and secured the Velcro strips tight around the matching booties. He stared through the clear visor at the four industrial space heaters. They were on wheels, situated around a battered wooden chair. A few feet away on the floor, sat a giant roll of bubble wrap and a large bottle of baby oil.

As he stepped into the light, shadows danced throughout the open space and crept up the cement walls. He clutched the rectangular remote control in his gloved hand and tapped one of the four red buttons.

One of the heaters clicked on and roared like a hurricane, as a brilliant, orange-reddish glow flashed through the front of the metal grill. A rat the size of an overstuffed kitten scampered by and disappeared into the darkness.

One by one, he turned on each of the heaters and watched the glow encircle the chair like spotlights being prepared for the main stage attraction to appear. Sweat streamed down the back of his neck, along his hairline, and dripped between his shoulders, soaking his T-shirt. His eyes roamed to the built-in metal cage, and then to the young woman sitting on the floor, hunched over, shivering, wearing only a black bra and panties. Adrenaline raced through his body. The woman lifted her arms and clutched the bars of the cage with both hands. She moaned as she tried to stand, but she was too weak from the Rohypnol he'd put in her drink.

She raised her trembling head. Strands of hair stuck to the side of her face. Terrified green eyes stared back at him through the bars, and he tasted her fear.

* * *

Victory's cell phone shrilled. She stirred in bed and eventually opened her eyes. Sunlight poked through the ends of the blinds. She squinted at the clock on the night table. It read 7:33. Groggy, she reached for her phone, answered the call, and closed her eyes again.

"Remember what Lynch said last night about turning your ringer off? That man's on to something," she said.

"Sadly, not possible in this business, Vic."

"Hmm. I'll be in around noon, Ryan. Tell that to anyone who asks, okay?"

"Says she'll be here in a few hours, sir."

Her eyes popped open. "What? Who are you talking to?"

"Victory, hi. Get your boots on now. A few hours is not going to cut it."

It was her boss, Joe Mains, agent-in-charge of the Cincinnati field office. His voice sounded pinched and edged with concern.

Victory jerked upright in bed. "The Wrapper? He didn't."

"He did. Late last night."

"Where?"

"Daniel Drake Park."

Her heart sank. She threw aside the feather duvet and scrambled to her feet. "Are you sure?"

"No doubt about it. Just got the call from Cincinnati homicide. Female, brunette, in her twenties," Mains said.

A shot of sympathy zapped through her veins for the unknown victim. Another young woman was dead at the hands of a demented monster.

"Damn it." She paced the bedroom in the dark, dressed in panties and a baggy T-shirt—the same shirt her husband wore the day before he had died. "He's never killed this close to the anniversary date. Something has set him off. A trigger. Something real or a paranoid delusion. But what?"

"Beats the hell out of me. The sick bastard has some deep issues going on. Maybe he's taunting us. Or worse... stepping it up."

Victory had her doubts. "There's been too long of a cooling-off period between kills for him to be stepping up his game."

Six months had passed since The Wrapper's last victim, and the tenth anniversary of his first kill was a couple of days away. There was a fifty-fifty chance he'd kill again on the anniversary unless he could be stopped before then. Victory was determined to be the one to put a stop to his murderous rampage.

Back in her Quantico days with the Behavioral Analysis Unit, she'd profiled numerous serial offenders. This guy was different. He wasn't a thrill killer and there wasn't any evidence of rape. No semen. That didn't mean his victims hadn't been sexually assaulted. By The Wrapper's sickening brutality these killings said, 'I'm going to erase you'. It was pure revenge.

"Well, I guess it's possible," she said to Mains, "but let's pray this isn't his new pattern, otherwise more women will turn up dead within days." Victory rummaged through her dresser drawers, pulled out a pair of black cargo pants, and a gray chenille sweater. She tossed them on the bed. "Has our team been notified?"

She wanted the ERT, the Bureau's Evidence Response Team, to work the scene as they had in the past. Consistency of the evidence collection was priority number one. They couldn't afford any screw-ups. Solving this case was too important to the Bureau, to the public, and to her.

"They're on their way. Ryan will already be there," Mains said.

"Be there in a half-hour." Victory ended the call and hurried into the bathroom. She turned on the sink faucet and splashed icy water on her face. After brushing her teeth, she twisted her long red hair into a ponytail and secured it with an elastic band.

While Victory dressed, the same disturbing questions played over in her mind. Why brunettes with green eyes in their twenties? What was the significance? A woman who'd rejected the killer in the past? A girlfriend? An overbearing or abusive mother? None of the victims knew each other. Their only connections were similar physical traits, and the killer had dumped the bodies in parks in Cincinnati and Cleveland. Her teeth sank into her lower lip. She didn't have the answer, let alone any evidence to work with, at least not yet.

In the bedroom, she opened her top dresser drawer, grabbed her leather hip holster, and put it on under her sweater. Instinctively she reached for her Glock 22 semi-automatic. Her throat constricted. Beside her weapon was the Carnegie Medal for acts of extraordinary heroism given to her for her husband after his death.

As much as she didn't want to think about Cleveland a year ago and, how her marriage had ended, tragically, it was always in the back of her mind like an open book stuck on the same page. Would she ever have the strength to turn the page?

"Don't allow the past to defeat you," the Bureau's shrink had said.

What did he know about loss anyway? He hadn't experienced her pain, loneliness, guilt, and anger. She stuffed her gun into her holster and closed the dresser drawer.

* * *

Thirty minutes later, Victory arrived at Daniel Drake Park. Her stomach clenched at the six inches of snow that had already fallen. The crime scene could be a disaster. She drew a heavy breath, exhaled, and got out of her vehicle. A stream of police vehicles and blue and red flashing lights lit the way while a police helicopter cir-cled like a predator, its bright searchlight sweeping the area.

She spotted Ryan talking to an elderly woman with her dog. The woman left as Victory approached.

"Disposed of in plain sight again, I hear."

Ryan glanced at her. "As many indignities as he could

think of. He's so, so angry."

"He could be just taunting us. Rubbing it in. Why girls with these specific features? Why always dumped in a park?"

Seven others. Gruesome images of their burnt bodies would forever be imprinted in her mind. She'd never forget the victim's names or the looks of sadness and loss on their loved one's faces.

"There's something to the fact he dumps some of them in Cleveland and the rest here. It's the only variation."

Clearly, his chosen dumping ground was significant to him. Why? Victory ran the killer's profile through her mind, a preliminary profile she'd put together based on the little she had to go on after The Wrapper's first three victims. The killer more than likely had resided in Ohio all his life, was at least six feet tall, in good physical shape, attractive, and the killings probably weren't motivated by sex.

"It's something," Victory said.

They walked together toward the police barricade.

"By the way, how's Jade doing these days?" Ryan asked.

He'd deliberately changed the subject to cut the tension, the nervous rush they always felt at a Wrapper crime scene, not sure what to expect, and hoping it wasn't worse than they'd imagined. They'd graduated from the academy together and she knew her partner well. Not only was Ryan like a brother, he was also her best friend. He'd even passed up a promotion in Cleveland to follow her to the Cincinnati Division after Josh had died.

"She's doing well. A typical twenty-three-year-old

enjoying college life. I can't wait to see her on my birthday. I miss the kid."

"It'll be good to see her." Ryan pointed. "Nice to see the damn media whores are out in full force."

A police barricade had been erected to hold back the onslaught of reporters. As Victory watched, the mob shifted to the right. Her muscles tightened. They'd been spotted.

Ryan glanced at her. "You ready?"

No. She detested the media, especially after Cleveland. Wasn't it enough she blamed herself for her husband's death?

"Let's do it." She inhaled an unsteady breath and let it out.

A young male reporter recognized Victory and raced toward her, shoving a microphone at her.

"Agent McClane, has the victim been identified? Are you any closer to catching The Wrapper?"

"Obviously, the investigation is in the preliminary stages. There's certainly nothing yet to indicate the same perpetrator is responsible."

"So, you think it might be a copycat?"

"I didn't say that either. We'll be having a press conference later, once we know more. Thank you." Victory pushed the microphone away and the reporter got the message to back off. They continued walking through the mob of reporters.

A male CNN reporter shouted, "Was the victim wrapped in bubble wrap like the others?"

Yes. And doused with baby oil and sedated with Rohypnol. Specific facts that only four people were aware of; Dr. Moore, Ryan, Detective Sean Brody, and herself. She had fiercely guarded those details because the last thing they needed was a psychotic copycat killer to deal with. Ignoring the question, Victory and Ryan kept moving. They'd almost made it to the far end of the barricade when a woman sprung silently from the shadows like a wild cat, with her cameraman.

Victory immediately recognized Melissa Mann, the obnoxious reporter from WKRC-News 1, dressed in a white faux-fur coat and matching hat with a large rhinestone tacked on the side. She looked like a glammed-out snow rabbit. Victory winced. This wasn't her first run-in with the reporter and it wouldn't be the last.

Ryan held out his arm to block the reporter. "No unauthorized personnel past the tapeline. You're well aware of that, Melissa."

Melissa ignored Ryan and held her ground. She thrust a wireless microphone in Victory's face. "It's been ten years and now eight victims, Agent McClane. People are terrified. Are you making any progress at all in The Wrapper case?"

The video camera was pointed at Victory, the red light on. *Don't lose it, McClane.* "I'll be making a public statement later, regarding this incident and how it may or may not relate to other crimes."

"What exactly is the FBI doing to end this? What are *you* doing, Agent McClane?"

She and Ryan brushed past the woman and flashed their IDs at one of the officers at the barricade.

The reporter didn't take the hint. Instead, she stayed a step behind, on their heels like a lost puppy. "Do you have any leads?"

Even if I did. I wouldn't tell you. Victory tried to keep her temper in check but failed. She spun and glared at the woman. "Look, Miss Mann. I understand you have a job to do. So, do I. Take another step and I'll have you both arrested."

The reporter stood speechless for a moment, her eyes wide, and then she laughed it off.

Victory and Ryan kept walking.

Ryan shook his head. "She's a lot of fun, isn't she?"

Victory rolled her eyes. "About as much fun as digging a sliver out of my finger."

Ahead, Victory spotted the top of a stone shelter shaped like a Unitarian Church. Bitter wind howled, and snow continued to fall and crunched under their feet. Portable lighting had been set up, and a tarp hung over the crime scene. The killer was getting bolder, continuing to evolve, and that worried her. He wanted the authorities to find the body. Why? Ryan handed her a pair of Nitrile gloves. She huddled in the warmth of her coat and put them on.

In the beginning, The Wrapper task force was comprised of six FBI agents, four local homicide detectives, and numerous liaison personnel. Not anymore. With manpower and resources spread thin nationwide since 9/11 and following the Boston Marathon terrorist attack, the force had dwindled to three. Her, Ryan, and Detective Sean Brody, a bear of a man with the Cincinnati Police Homicide Unit.

After trudging up an incline, Sean greeted them with a grim expression on his face. "Ryan. Vic." He shook his head. "Gotta warn you guys, this one is even worse than the last."

Images of The Wrapper's last victim were fresh in Victory's mind. She sighed, unable to imagine how it could be worse. "Good to know. The tenth anniversary of his first kill is only a few days away. Did he decide to do it early, or is there more to come?"

Neither man replied as they walked together to the crime scene.

In the light, Sean's eyes held a hardness, a side effect of the job. "A patrol officer got the call about seven-fifteen. Couple of teens called it in. The officer arrived at seven-twenty-five and secured the scene until her supervisor arrived."

Victory felt some relief, knowing the scene had been preserved. Bright yellow tape snapped in the wind, attached to stakes hammered into the ground. The smell of fresh snow mingled with burnt flesh. The crisp air reeked of death.

"Where are the teens now?" Victory asked.

Sean pointed to a police van nearby. "In there, still being questioned."

"I'll want to talk to them, too."

Sean nodded. "You two ready for this?"

Victory fought to keep her eyes open against the brutal wind and driving snow. "Ready."

Ryan nodded.

Dr. Moore from the Hamilton County Coroner's Office, a man with a quiet voice and a passionate appetite, was on his knees inches from the body. He placed paper bags over the victim's hands and secured them with rubber bands to preserve any possible evidence.

He looked up. "Hello, Victory. It's good to see you. Wish it was under different circumstances, though."

"Me too, Gregory." Even though he was a huge man and looked like he could crush someone with his bare hands, Dr. Moore had the disposition of a pussycat. This job just didn't seem to fit his nature.

She bent over the body. The nude female had been

left in a snowdrift, in a partial sitting position, her jaw wide, locked forever in a horrifying scream. Her nose was pretty much gone, except for bone. Greasy brown hair covered an empty eye socket. Bile crept up Victory's throat. *Breathe, McClane.* She stepped back and composed herself.

"You were right to prepare us, Sean."

"No one could ever be fully prepared to see something like that."

"The killer's rage is escalating. Something set him off," she said.

Victory swallowed hard and tried not to think about the pain and suffering the woman must have endured. What little skin was left on the victim's body glistened under the lights. Charred remains of what appeared to be bubble wrap were embedded in her shoulder, legs, and chest. Just like the others. The only lead they had from the beginning was the bubble wrap used by the killer, but the same wrap was used by thousands of stores, moving companies, and postal outlets throughout the country. Their only lead, useless. Sooner or later, The Wrapper would make a mistake.

Victory glanced away from the corpse and spotted Ryan speaking with one of their ERT techs. By the tension in her partner's jaw, their guys hadn't found anything useful that could identify or lead them to the killer.

"Cooked alive. See here?" Gregory pointed to the victim's right breast. "Looks like gummy silicone gel. I think our girl had breast implants. Getting a serial number from it could be difficult but –"

"It's worth a shot," Victory said.

Then she'd have to notify the victim's family. Days like this, she really hated her job.

He climbed to his feet and stripped off his gloves. "She hasn't been here long, relatively speaking. There's rigor mortis only in the small muscles. Time of death, close to midnight, I'd say. Give or take. I'll know more after the post-mortem."

"Thanks, Gregory. Let's hope we finally get a solid lead."

His eyes darkened with sadness. "Pray we do."

Little did he know, she had prayed every day since her squad supervisor had designated her case-agent-in-charge of the investigation. She was the shit deflector, the one who took all the heat from her superiors, the media, and the public.

"Well, I'm going to grab a smoke. She's all yours, Victory," Gregory said.

He walked past her and lit a cigarette. An arctic gust of wind sent a chill down her spine. Victory stared at the victim's remaining green eye, and it seemed to be staring back at her accusingly.

CHAPTER FOUR

One night. Two victims. Unlucky was an understatement, especially for Eddie Bullington and Jane Doe spread open on stainless-steel tables in the morgue.

Victory didn't want to think about the mountain of paperwork ahead, or the news conference she needed to schedule for this afternoon. Not to mention the worst task of all, notifying Jane Doe's family once they had an ID. The thought twisted and turned inside her. Thankfully, Sean was contacting Eddie Bullington's next-of-kin.

Armed with egg and bacon burritos and two extra-large coffees from the Blue Devil diner down the street, she rushed inside the field office doors on Ronald Reagan Drive. A swoosh of frosty air trailing behind her. After checking in with security, she took the elevator to the third floor.

At two-thirty in the afternoon, the four-storey concrete and glass building was buzzing with organized chaos. Maneuvering through the maze of cubicles, she found Ryan busy at his workstation, the tips of his unruly blond hair still damp from the snow. He looked as tired and frustrated as she felt.

She plopped the bag of burritos and a coffee on his desk. "You and your damn coin tosses. I froze my ass off out there."

Ryan rocked back in the chair and shot her a crooked grin. "Guess you should have picked tails." He opened the bag, grabbed two burritos, and handed her one as if it were a peace offering.

"Smartass." After setting her breakfast on her own desk, she unzipped her coat and fingered through her messages. One caught her attention.

I need to talk with you. Please call me. It's important.
Melissa
513-452-6791

She scanned the rest of the messages. "Do you believe this? Three messages already this morning from Melissa Mann. Thank God she doesn't have my cell number."

Ryan shrugged and grinned. "Maybe Melissa wants to be your new BFF."

Victory rolled her eyes. "Not in this lifetime or any other. That woman is such a pain in the ass." She crumpled the messages and tossed them into the wastebasket. Settling behind her desk, she forced herself to eat, knowing she'd need as much energy as possible to get through the day.

"I checked NCIC. No one matching our Jane Doe's description has been reported missing yet," Ryan said.

The National Crime Information Center's database was one of many resources they used to track criminal records, fugitives, the missing, unidentified persons, and other crime-related information. Everything inside her went still and cold. The young woman had family somewhere. She was someone's daughter, sister, friend. She should have had a lifetime ahead of her.

Victory tried to ignore the anger tightening in her stomach. "She's got family somewhere, a friend. I'm sure we'll get a match soon. Young women don't exist in a vacuum."

She wanted nothing more than to catch the killer. She logged onto her computer, determined to get a head-start on her paperwork. Distributing information about both cases to the participating law enforcement agencies and the prosecutor's office was a top priority.

Angie Marston, their liaison between the local cops and media relations supervisor for the field office, stopped at Ryan's workstation. "Morning. Looks like you two have seen better days."

Ryan ogled the angelic blonde. "There are other things I'd much rather be doing." His gaze moved to her shoulders, then to her breasts.

Angie smiled coyly.

The thick sexual tension in the air pulsated with electric currents. If inter-office romances weren't frowned upon, Ryan and Angie would have hooked up the moment they met five years earlier. Victory was convinced the two were secretly seeing each other after hours anyway.

"You guys seen this?" Angie looked away from Ryan long enough to hand Victory a copy of the *Cincinnati Enquirer*.

Victory took a sip of her coffee. Frustration swelled, and she shook her head as she read the three-inch head-line:

WRAPPER CLAIMS VICTIM NUMBER EIGHT.
Cincinnati's serial killer causing citywide fear similar

to the Cincinnati Strangler panic in the 1960s...

"That should calm any panic," she said wryly.

Over the course of The Wrapper investigation, the newspapers annoyed her with dramatic, copy-selling headlines, and the television networks hadn't been much better. They'd recruited self-declared experts who offered their opinions on a case they weren't officially involved with. No wonder she disliked the media so much. Most of the time they were more of a hindrance to justice than anything else.

"Check out the other story." Angie pointed to the newspaper.

Further down the page, Victory scanned the second major story of the day:

CONTROVERSIAL RADIO HOST FOUND DEAD.
Sources close to the investigation confirm Eddie Bullington's death being investigated by the FBI.

Victory passed the paper to Ryan.

He gave it a quick read then tossed it on his desk. "Could've been worse. At least they haven't caught wind of the magical mystery killer. Imagine the fun they'd have with The Shadow."

That should have been reassuring, but it wasn't. Information leaks happened more than Victory cared to admit, and once the news hit about The Shadow, her run-ins with the media would be a circus.

"Oh, they'll find out, soon enough, I imagine." She nodded to Angie. "Angie, please schedule a press conference for four-thirty. Also, find out who's in charge of Eddie Bullington's hate-crime investigation. Thanks."

"Sure thing." Angie turned and strutted back toward

her desk at the far end of the office.

Ryan's gaze was glued to the woman's backside.

Victory always found it amusing the way the woman wiggled her hips clearly for his benefit.

She shook her head. "Hey, partner. You think we can get some work done now?"

"Yeah, yeah. Sorry, Vic." He scarfed down his burrito in a few bites, crumpled the wrapper, and tossed it, free-throw-style, into the wastebasket beside him.

Victory stood, scooped up two files folders from her desk, and grabbed her coffee. She looked at what was left of her burrito, her appetite pretty much gone.

Ryan followed her into what was known as 'The Death Room'. Victory closed the door.

The room was divided by fixed whiteboards, bulletin boards, and two wall maps. The left side of the room was devoted to The Wrapper, and the right side was for The Shadow case. A series of thick books containing all the pertinent investigative information were stacked on tables on each side of the room.

While Ryan checked the fax machine, Victory uncapped a black marker, wrote Jane Doe on one of the whiteboards, and Eddie Bullington on the other. Her thoughts veered back to Bullington's bedroom.

Something *had* touched her cheek. It wasn't her imagination. She admitted to herself that she'd been tired and knew that could often have odd effects on the senses, but no; she knew what she had felt. It was real, in some way. It wasn't a bug. More like breath against her skin, but no one was near her. A shiver drove up her spine. Now she was just creeping herself out.

"This is going to sound off the wall," she said, "but— when we were in Bullington's house it felt as if someone or something was there with us, observing. It just felt... weird."

"Now you're really losing it, Vic. You've never been into that paranormal crap. Might as well jump on the Bullington paranoia wagon while you're there. It's exhaustion, nothing more."

She was quiet for a long moment. "Yeah. You're probably right." Her gaze traveled to the whiteboards. "Two murders from two high-profile cases in one night. We're just lucky as hell, huh?"

Ryan nodded and handed her a fax. "Ballistics confirmed that the gun found at the scene is the gun used to kill Bullington."

No surprise there. She thought about The Shadow's previous victim, Steven Rothman, victim number fifteen, owner of the largest pharmaceutical company in the country. His eleven-year-old daughter had called 9-1-1 because "her daddy wouldn't come out of the bathroom". While relaxing in the tub, his throat had been slashed from ear to ear with his own straight razor. The bathroom door was locked from the inside and the room had no windows. At first glance, it had appeared Rothman had taken his own life, but the razor was found in a closed drawer on the other side of the bathroom. No prints were on the weapon, only the victim's blood. The man couldn't have slit his throat, got out of the tub, made it across the room to put the razor back and cleaned up the water and blood on the floor before bleeding out. The evidence response team had sprayed the bathroom with Luminol and only found blood in the bathtub and blood splatter and spray on the wall next to the tub. Even if it were possible, there would've been evidence. There was none.

"Twenty years this bastard has been toying with us," Victory said.

"There's no way he could get into Bullington's place, never mind get upstairs and into that room."

Victory frowned. She had no clue. "It still could be something normal. Someone with specific skills, experience with security systems, and the know-how to bypass them."

Ryan looked skeptical. "And be able to hack into Alternate's elaborate system without the company knowing. From what Lynch told us, that doesn't seem too likely. I'll give them a call and get a list of the past and present employees. On the off-chance."

"It's a place to start anyway."

Victory didn't believe they would discover anything and she knew Ryan didn't either. It was the only theory she could come up with at this point, though. They needed more facts.

While Ryan made the call, Victory sipped her coffee and eyed the bulletin board lined with photographs of each of The Shadow's victims.

They were all well-known for whatever reason, good or bad, and in the public eye, including Eddie Bullington. Was that why they were targeted? It just didn't make sense. What were they missing?

Her phone rang. The high-pitched sound made her flinch. She pulled the phone from her pocket and noticed the screen displayed the coroner's number. "Good morning, Gregory."

"We got lucky, Victory. We managed to get a serial number from one of the breast implants and traced it to a local cosmetic surgeon. I've got an ID for you."

"Shoot." She snatched a pen and paper from the desk

and jotted down the information.

"12981 Dickens Avenue."

The street name sounded familiar, then it hit her. "That's only a couple of blocks from where her body was dumped," she said, more to herself than to him.

Dr. Moore continued. "I already notified her mother. She's on her way in."

She glanced at Ryan, still on the phone with the security company. "We'll be there in thirty. Thanks, Gregory."

"Wait, Victory. There is something else you need to know." A long pause of airy silence on the other end of the line. "Nicole Henderson was eight weeks pregnant."

CHAPTER FIVE

The news of Nicole Henderson's pregnancy traveled through Victory like a high-voltage shock wave. She dropped her cell phone on the desk, relieved that the screen didn't break. The Wrapper had to be stopped. The monster had killed an innocent child. *A death sentence would be too easy for him.* She wanted to see the killer spend the rest of his life in solitary confinement, as his body and mind withered and wasted away.

"What's wrong?" Ryan asked.

"We got an ID on our Jane Doe. Her name is Nicole Henderson, twenty-four years old." She paused for a moment "Ryan. She was eight weeks pregnant."

His jaw tightened, and his eyes turned dark, a look she'd only seen once before—the day her husband had been killed.

"It wasn't enough to torture and murder her. Sick bastard."

Sick was one way to put it. Victory stared at the bulletin board filled with grotesque photographs of The Wrapper's victims, each numbered with black marker displayed in gory detail. These women meant nothing to the killer. They were objects. *Things.* He tortured and punished them for something that had happened in his life. Whatever that trigger was, it had escalated his rage. There was nothing worse than a pissed off serial killer. No one was safe. Victory didn't know the killer's motive or his personal agenda, but she knew what she had to do. She needed to get inside his head and figure out what made him tick before he struck again.

While Ryan dispatched their evidence team, Victory called Sean. He answered on the third ring.

"Brody."

"Sean, where are you?"

"I'm heading east on Ross Avenue. I just finished up with Sarah Halberd, Bullington's sister. She didn't seem too surprised by his death. She's convinced the NSM finally got to him."

"It's probably better if she believes that, at least until we have more to go on."

Everything had a logical explanation. Whoever had killed Bullington was highly intelligent and methodical. Even though Victory was sure The Shadow was responsible, she wasn't going to fall into the tunnel-vision trap.

"Is there anyone who might financially benefit from his death?" she asked.

"Not so far. His wife died of cancer last year. No kids. His parents are deceased."

"An associate or girlfriend, perhaps?"

"I'll keep digging."

"Thanks, Sean. Also, we just got an ID on our Jane Doe. I need you to meet our team at 12981 Dickens Avenue, while Ryan and I speak with the victim's mother."

"Do you think The Wrapper killed her there?"

"Not likely. He needs a place where he can feel safe,

somewhere he can spend time with his victim and have complete privacy. A busy residential area wouldn't work for him. If the techs turn up anything, let me know."

Solving both cases would boil down to victimology. The more Victory knew about the victims, the more she'd learn about the killer.

❋ ❋ ❋

Victory and Ryan entered through the back door of the Hamilton County Coroner's office on Eden Avenue. The overcrowded cube-like brick building was built in the early '70s when computers were a big-ticket novelty, and DNA identification was stuff you'd see in a science fiction movie. Victory knew Gregory would be happy when the new multi-million-dollar coroner's office and crime lab opened around the corner.

"Do you think he knew she was pregnant?" Ryan asked.

What if he had? What if The Wrapper had changed his victimology because his usual profile wasn't enough anymore?

A shiver spidered up her spine. "I doubt it, but we both know human behavior isn't set in stone."

"He killed a growing baby. Wait till the media finds out. Christ, Vic. I can already picture the headlines."

Years of constant media attention had everyone's nerves frazzled. So far, eight families had been torn apart because of The Wrapper. Victory's stomach gurgled and knotted. "I don't even want to think about it."

"I bet he's following the media reports real close, all proud of himself."

"Serial murderers often do. They take immense

pride in their actions."

After entering Gregory's cramped office, Victory sat next to a defeated-looking woman in her mid-forties with long stylish blonde hair. She was clutching a framed photograph in one hand and a wad of crumpled tissues in the other.

Gregory was sitting behind his cluttered desk. A jumble of office supplies and stacks of file folders covered the top. An open bookcase was crammed with thick medical books.

"Mrs. Henderson, this is Agent McClane and Agent Slater. They're here to speak to you about Nicole."

Victory took a seat next to the distraught woman. Ryan sat on the other side. "Our condolences, Mrs. Henderson."

Tears flowed down Lorene Henderson's cheeks and dripped onto her white blouse. She looked at Victory. "I want to see my daughter."

Victory's heart ached. *You don't want to see what that monster did to her. You don't want to remember your child that way.*

"I have to advise against it because of the condition of the body," Dr. Moore said, his voice soft and compassionate.

He'd been with the coroner's office for thirty years and was more than experienced in handling victims' loved ones.

"I see that you brought a photograph of Nicole," Gregory said. "She was a beautiful young woman."

Lorene peered down at the picture and pride fought through damp eyes. "Yes, she is, isn't she?"

Victory noticed how the grieving mother spoke in past and present tense, her mind clouded with shock and disbelief. Victory had done the same thing when she learned her husband had been killed.

Dr. Moore slid a form and pen across his desk. "I need you to sign this release, so we can have Nicole transferred to the Taylor Funeral Home as you requested."

The woman reached and took the pen. Her hand shook as she signed her name. "I don't understand how this could have happened." She took a deep, tremulous breath. "A serial killer? The one in the newspaper?"

"I'm sorry. I know how difficult this is," Victory said. *More than you know.* "But we need to ask you some questions." She touched the woman's arm gently. "Anytime you need to stop, let us know."

Lorene lifted her chin and dabbed her eyes with a tissue. "Okay."

Victory paused for a long moment and swallowed the hard lump in her throat. "Did your daughter live alone?"

"She moved into her own place last May. Maybe if she hadn't moved out…"

She understood Lorene's guilt, and how she desperately needed answers. There was nothing Victory could say or do to make the woman feel better. Instead, she had to continue to learn as much as she could if she had any hope of stopping The Wrapper.

"Did Nicole have a boyfriend, someone she'd been seeing on a regular basis?"

"Not that I know of. She's extremely busy at work."

Nicole had been seeing someone. Someone had fathered her child. Maybe the women didn't have a tight mother-daughter relationship?

"Where did your daughter work?" Ryan asked.

"At Omicron. She was a video game designer. Nicole

loved working for Mr. Lynn. He's a great boss. Always very supportive and made Nicole feel special." Lorene sniffed and blew her nose. "Nicole loved her job. She was thrilled when she landed the position with Daryl. No, sorry, Derrick."

Victory and Ryan exchanged glances.

"Derrick Lynn? The son of the Secretary of Defense?" Victory asked.

Lorene nodded absently.

Ryan shifted in the chair. "How long has she worked at Omicron?"

"For almost four years. She was working on the sequel to a game. One all the kids played, she told me." Lorene shook her head. "But for the life of me, I can't remember the name."

"Was it Black Magic Island?" Victory asked. She was familiar with some of the popular fantasy role-playing games her own daughter had played over the years.

"No, it had something to do with dragons, I think. Dragon's Breath?

"Dragon's Drought?"

"Yes. That's the one."

"When did you see Nicole last?"

"Two days ago." Lorene's eyes started to mist over again. "She'd come home for supper and a visit. I made her favorite. Grilled salmon, scalloped potatoes, and cherry cheesecake." She looked down at her hands and twisted her fingers in her lap. "Did she suffer? Please, I need to know."

Victory's throat tightened, and she could taste the tension in the room. "No." She lied, unable to tell the grieving mother the sickening truth.

The truth was Nicole Henderson had suffered an unspeakably painful death. For whatever reason, the serial killer had soaked the young woman in baby oil, wrapped her in bubble wrap, and then burnt her to death using some type of torch or heating device.

"Where's Nicole's father?" Ryan asked.

"Jake passed away five years ago. Heart attack. He was a good man."

Victory's heart sank. Could this get any worse? The woman had lost so much. "Do you have any other children?"

"No. Nicole was an only child." Lorene lowered her head. "Now she's gone."

Victory didn't want to ask but had to. "Was your daughter wearing any jewelry?"

"Her father had given her a white gold band with her initials engraved inside when she'd graduated from college. She wore it all the time. He was so proud of her. The ring meant the world to her. I'd like it back, please."

Victory glanced at Gregory.

He shook his head.

The Wrapper had likely taken the ring as a trophy, just like he had taken a piece of jewelry from all his other victims.

Victory's muscles tensed. "I'm afraid we didn't find a ring."

"What?" A long pause of silence. "Did the killer take it?"

"We think he may have."

Lorene couldn't hide the pain in her eyes.

Damn it. All the woman wanted was a small piece of her daughter to hold on to. Something. Anything. Victory couldn't even give her that and things were about to get worse.

She inhaled a steadying breath and exhaled, steeling herself for the toughest question she had to ask the grieving mother. "Mrs. Henderson, did you know your daughter was pregnant?"

Lorene sat silent. Her knuckles turned white, clutching the photograph to her chest. "I was going to be a grandmother?" She stared off for a long moment and swallowed. "Was it a girl or boy?"

The room went tensely quiet. Victory looked across the desk to Dr. Moore for the answer.

His gaze lowered to one of many reports on his desk then back to the distraught woman. "A girl. I'm terribly sorry."

Her bottom lip quivered. Tears flowed again, and the mother sobbed uncontrollably.

The scene was heartbreaking. In a five-year span, Lorene Henderson had lost a husband, daughter, and granddaughter.

Not wanting to upset the grief-stricken woman anymore, Victory stood. "I think that's all for now. I'm truly sorry for your loss."

When Victory was about to walk out the door, Lorene grabbed her hand. "Promise me you'll find who did this to Nicole and my grandchild."

Without thinking, the words slipped through her lips. "I promise." She knew better than to promise something she may not be able to deliver. But she'd felt a bond with the woman. A deep connection to her pain and loss. The same heart-crushing agony she had felt when she'd lost Josh.

In the corridor, Victory booted the bottom of the wall. "God damn it. I need to find that bastard. You heard her, Ryan. She's lost everything. Her daughter, a grand-

44 | KIM CRESSWELL

child, her husband. Everyone."

Seconds went by before her partner said anything. She could tell he was choosing his words carefully.

"I saw it in your eyes back there. That anger. You still blame yourself for Cleveland. It wasn't your fault, Vic. Frank Sanders chose to rob the First National Bank that day. Frank Sanders killed Josh. Seventeen people were saved that day."

But not my husband. Not the person who meant everything to me.

Immediately after Josh's death, Victory had requested a transfer out of the Cleveland office to the Cincinnati Division.

Tears gathered behind her eyes and that's where they'd stay, hidden from the world. Always. "But not Josh. A damn medal is hardly a replacement for my husband." She blinked hard and looked away.

"I miss him too, Vic. He was a good guy. The best. But we can't save everyone. It doesn't work that way. Finding this sick sonofabitch will never make up for losing Josh."

Her partner's words pricked her skin and hurt even more because he was right.

She wanted to find The Wrapper for her own selfish reasons. Not, primarily, for the victims. Not for their families. Somehow in her mind, as insane as the thought was, she believed finding the serial killer would help make up for her loss.

As they walked to the rear exit, Victory's boots echoed heavily on the floor. She silently cursed herself. Her twisted logic sounded even more irrational the longer she thought about it.

At the end of the hallway, a morgue attendant pushed a stainless-steel gurney with a corpse into one of the autopsy rooms. The automatic glass doors swooshed closed behind him and she caught the scent of strong antiseptic mixed with the underlying stench of death and decomposition.

Death was all around her. She couldn't get away from it. At that moment, anger turned to determination and Victory made a vow. She had to find The Wrapper before he killed again.

CHAPTER SIX

In his ninth-floor office, Derrick sat behind his desk and leaned back in his chair. By mid-morning, a headache drilled through his temples. What did his contact want? The question echoed stronger in his head. Requesting a face-to-face was out of character to the point of being worrisome. For the most part, communication between the two men was conducted via encrypted email before and after a target was eliminated. The man rarely left Virginia, let alone had time to visit for a one-on-one meeting. They didn't have that kind of relationship. Not like some fathers and sons. And, since his contact was the Secretary of Defense, Derrick wondered how he would even find the time for a visit. Two loud raps on his office door interrupted his thoughts.

Bob Riley, his production manager, strutted in, slugging back an energy drink. He was in his early fifties, five-ten, about three inches shorter than Derrick, and had a serious addiction to highly-caffeinated energy drinks. He stopped in front of the desk with a file folder tucked under his arm.

Derrick picked up a pen and rolled it through his fingers. "Are we on schedule?"

Bob plunked down across from him in one of the leather tub chairs. By the dark circles under the man's eyes, Derrick knew the answer. They were.

"Dragon's Drought, The Homecoming, will premiere right on time next Wednesday at midnight." He tossed the folder to Derrick and continued. "The number-guys have revised their estimate from ten to fifteen million online players within the first twelve hours. It's gonna be incredible. Pre-sales are already astronomical."

Months of hype surrounding the release of the sequel to Dragon's Drought had sent Oricrom's stock to the moon. The company's shareholders were elated. So was Derrick. He flipped open the manila folder and scanned the projected cash flow report. "Fantastic. This is great. It doesn't get much better than this."

"Get this. Online Gamer magazine named Dragon's Drought, The Homecoming, the most anticipated online multiplayer game of the decade." Bob grinned and rubbed his hands together. "Double cha-ching."

Derrick was proud of what he'd accomplished. He'd made a comfortable legal living for himself. He'd started the gaming company the same year he'd signed on with the government. It was a believable cover, all part of the show, a façade to ensure his true occupation remained hidden. He had handpicked the best graphic artists, animators, and programmers from around the country and beyond, including some very creative local talent to develop his fantasy role-playing games.

Derrick smiled and noticed Bob's fingers began to fidget in his lap, a side effect of the energy drink. "I know how hard everyone has worked on this project. Especially you, Bob. Is Liz still busting your balls over the long hours?"

"Nope, thanks to you. Not a peep out of her since she got her hands on my bonus check. She's out shopping for a new dress for the release party. I don't want to see the bill for that one. You know, shoes, purse, and whatever else she can think of. Which reminds me, I caught up with Jenna. She's done wrapping up the last-minute details with The Kennedy Heights Art Center. It's going to be one hell of a bash." He hopped out of the chair, grabbed his empty can, and crushed it in his hand. "Anyway, I need to run a few things by advertising. I'll catch up with you later."

After Bob left, Derrick's secretary stopped inside the door with a bewildered expression on her face. She closed the door behind her. In the years she'd worked for him, Derrick had never seen the woman look so rattled.

He straightened in the chair. "What's wrong, Katherine?"

"I told the FBI you were in a meeting, but Agent McClane said she's not leaving until she speaks with you. Is everything alright, Derrick?"

Agent McClane was all he heard. It was as if the air had been sucked out of his lungs. It took a few seconds to get his bearings. Why was she here? "Give me a few minutes." Derrick fought to keep his voice even. "Then send her in."

His secretary gave him a *you're-not-going-to-tell-me-what's-going-on* look and left the office. Her heels clicked noisier than usual down the corridor toward the reception area.

He stood, and stared through the panoramic windows at the city, his nerve endings on high alert. Light snow fell. In the distance, he could barely see the Purple People Bridge.

Why was McClane here?

Cold tunneled deep in his gut, twisting, and gnawing. The most dangerous possibility—she knew his secret. Impossible. Unless she was psychic, which he doubted. Had his contact requested a meeting concerned the FBI knew something? He hoped not. As far as he knew, no one suspected him in Bullington's death or any of the other deaths during the past twenty years. How could they? His paranormal abilities made his actions untraceable, impossible for his astral body to leave any physical evidence, exactly why the government had recruited him in the first place. He was a ghost. A shadow, according to the FBI.

After eliminating the radio host, Derrick had returned to the man's bedroom, his astral body hovering, watching Victory. He could have easily freaked her out even more and made her think she was losing her mind by moving the shell casing on the floor, or by setting off the security system. But he didn't. Instead, years of curiosity had gotten the best of him. He'd felt her flinch and shiver, a spark of awareness when he had exhaled against her cheek. He rammed his hands into the pockets of his jeans. He'd made a mistake. Crossed the line. Something he'd never done in the past and could never do again. Now she was here wanting to speak with him.

"Thanks for seeing us," Victory said.

Derrick heard her smoky, smooth voice. He turned, slow and deliberate, not wanting to appear anxious. She was even more stunning in person. "What can I do for you?"

He knew he was staring but couldn't help himself. Her features weren't fuzzy and distorted like he'd witnessed while etheric traveling. He'd seen her on TV, of course, but that still didn't do her justice. In a glance, he took in her sculptured cheekbones, soft full mouth, and fiery red hair pulled back in a loose ponytail, hanging past her shoulders.

Good-looking or not, Derrick had no illusions as to what he was. Something Agent McClane could never discover.

✳   ✳   ✳

Victory was so distracted by the man's looks, she couldn't stop staring, entranced by his intense blue eyes and hair the color of burnt hot chocolate, with slivers of silver at his temples. He was distinguished-looking and gorgeous. Then he smiled. Spikes of warmth surged through her body, and her breath caught as if air was unable to make it to her lungs. She'd never experienced such raw and primitive attraction to a man before. Not even when she had met Josh.

Ryan cleared his throat and gave her a gentle snap-out-of-it-nudge in the ribs with his elbow.

What was she thinking? She mentally slapped herself and forced herself to focus on the business at hand.

Derrick moved from the window and leaned against the front of his desk. He was dressed in jeans and a white dress shirt with the sleeves rolled up to his forearms.

She knew he was looking at her even though she tried to keep her gaze glued toward the desk.

"What can I do for you?" Derrick asked.

"We need to ask you a few questions, Mr. Lynn," Ryan said.

He was watching her, probably grinning at the way she was acting. Thank God, Ryan decided to take the lead because her mouth wasn't working. Victory remained standing and caught the scent of Derrick's aftershave: spicy musk and sandalwood. He smelled as good as he looked. She wasn't going to get any closer to the man. Two feet away was plenty close enough. *Focus, McClane.*

No matter how attracted she was to Derrick, her gaze instinctively traveled to his face. She needed to witness his reaction, decipher, read between the lines.

His eyebrows rose. "Sure. Questions about what?"

"One of your employees. Nicole Henderson," Ryan said.

"Nicole? Is everything alright?"

"She was found dead last night."

Derrick gasped. "Dead? My God. What happened?"

Victory slid her hands into her coat pockets and studied him. He appeared puzzled as if he had been waiting to hear something different. Interesting. She made a mental note. His eyes were wide, and he had a glazed look of shock on his face. Was his reaction genuine? It was too early to tell. She wasn't about to get into details about Nicole's death. He'd learn enough through the media. Everyone would.

Victory finally found her voice. "I'm sorry. We can't discuss particulars of an ongoing investigation. When did you last see Nicole?"

He paused for a second before answering. "I think it was yesterday afternoon during my meeting with the design department." Derrick shook his head. "I can't believe this. Her mother must be devastated."

Ryan's cell phone buzzed. He yanked it out of his coat pocket and looked at the screen. "I need to take this." He glanced at her, then rushed out of the office.

The worst timing in the world. She was alone with Derrick. Her eyes shifted to the leather couch situated to her left, then to the black and glass coffee table that matched Derrick's desk. As if he was sensing her discomfort, Derrick motioned to the chair in front of him.

"Please. Have a seat, Agent McClane."

"I'm fine, thank you." Victory fiddled with the zipper on her coat. *You're a professional. Act like one.* "How well did you know Nicole?"

"She had an integral spot here. We worked together a lot."

"Always just business?"

His jaw tightened then he laughed. "Of course. Are you implying something? I'm twice her age."

"And how old is that?" She wanted to kick herself for asking.

"Forty-five and old enough to know better. If anything, you're more my type."

He smiled again, his teeth ridiculously white. Victory had the sudden urge to flee the room. But she had a job to do. She needed answers if she was going to stop The Wrapper.

"That's hardly appropriate, Mr. Lynn. Would you be willing to take a DNA test?"

"Sure."

Agreeing to the test had surprised her. He hadn't hesitated for even a second to think about it. Victory felt confident he wasn't the father of Nicole's baby. If Derrick wasn't, then who was?

She drew a relieved breath, confused as to why she was relieved. "Where were you last night, Mr. Lynn?"

"Here, till about nine. I grabbed some takeout sushi on the way home. Got there about ten. I'm happy to provide access to any camera or anything else that verifies that."

"Was Nicole dating anyone at work?"

"Not that I know of. She did get on quite well with Jason Williams, one of our animators. He'll be on the second floor, in the animation studio. Listen, I'd like to cover the funeral expenses for Mrs. Henderson. Anything I can do to help."

"That's very nice of you, Mr. Lynn." Was the man offering out of the goodness of his heart, or out of guilt because he was hiding something? He was making her very nervous and she didn't like it.

"I hope it's not too insensitive, considering the timing, but...have dinner with me."

Victory was totally caught off guard. Heat flushed her cheeks. She didn't answer, couldn't, for what seemed like minutes. "Yes, that's totally insensitive."

"You're right. I'm sorry. It's just—"

She pulled a business card from her coat pocket and handed it to him. "Call us if you think of anything that might help the investigation."

Derrick took the card. His fingers brushed hers.

Her pulse pounded erratically. His touch seemed familiar, but she'd never met the man before today. Very odd. She snapped her hand away and left the room feeling a little disoriented, her mind hazy, foggy.

In the hallway, she almost bumped into Ryan.

"Hey, that was Sean. Nothing worthwhile turned up at Nicole's house and no sign of a struggle."

Just as Victory had expected. "He wouldn't kill her there. He needs somewhere he can feel safe and comfortable."

"But where?"

Victory shrugged.

"What happened in there, Vic?"

Victory wasn't going to tell her partner that Derrick had asked her out for dinner. She'd already made herself look like a drooling idiot. "I don't think he's the father or has anything to do with her death. There are a few things we need to check out, though. It felt as if he were hiding something."

"I'm not talking about that, Vic. Nothing wrong with being attracted to someone, but it came close to affecting your professionalism."

She felt a surge of guilt. She had no right being attracted to Derrick or any man. It was far too soon. She was on an emotional roller-coaster ride and sex was not part of the mix, but twenty-one years of marriage had spoiled her. She missed her husband—wanted him back. Damn it. She was lonely.

"I don't want to talk about it, and I wonder if you know how insulting that was."

"Sorry, but—"

She held up one hand. "How about we focus on the two serial killers out there."

One thing was certain. Derrick came off too cool and had all the right answers. What was he hiding?

CHAPTER SEVEN

After Victory left, Derrick paced his office and cursed under his breath. He had asked an FBI agent out for dinner. His gut tightened. He'd spent twenty years staying under the radar. What had gotten into him? There was something about Victory, something he couldn't shake. A vulnerability poking through a rough and confident exterior.

She was dangerous. The enemy. He eliminated enemies.

He didn't like using the words kill or murder. He protected humanity. Eliminated threats and helped to defend the security of the United States. It's what his grandfather had done, what his father had done. He was no different than a CIA-hired contractor, part of a secret government program used to locate and assassinate enemies during Nazi Germany or Vietnam.

Derrick stopped behind his desk and looked out the window as the sun made a brief appearance before disappearing for the day.

He had made two critical errors within twenty-four hours involving a woman, the same woman who could put him behind bars for the rest of his life if she discovered his secret. He had to fix the problem, make his mistakes work to his advantage. If he kept a close eye on Victory, he'd know what she was up to and if she had anything on him. The plan sounded simple but he knew it wouldn't be. Then his thoughts shifted to Nicole. He needed to get all the employees together and let them know what had happened. He couldn't imagine the pain Nicole's mother must be feeling. A very sad situation.

Derrick was about to buzz his secretary when his cell phone rang. He plucked the phone off the desk and checked the caller ID. It was his father. He answered, confident the DoD had employed their technology to guarantee a secure line. "Hi, Dad."

"Son, I'll be in town in a few hours. Meet me at your house."

His father's tone was abrupt and rushed—the usual, from a man who'd spent most of his life in the United States Air Force before working for the Department of Defense.

Again, Derrick wondered why his father was making the lengthy drive instead of contacting him by email. "What's going on?"

There was a long beat of silence on the other end before his father said, "It's urgent."

✻   ✻   ✻

Victory wanted to be anywhere but here. The FBI press conference room was hot and cramped, much like the rest of the office space. Rows of chairs extended the width of the room overcrowded with reporters. There was no surprise when she spotted Melissa Mann, sitting front and center dressed in a tailored navy jacket, matching short skirt, and thigh-high black leather boots. The reporter had already left three messages and, so far, Victory had been able to duck the pesky woman. But luck would run out eventually. It always did.

While she waited for the press conference to begin, Victory couldn't get Derrick out of her head. She was still angry at herself for acting unprofessionally in front of her partner. She'd acted like a complete idiot. What was wrong with her?

Between the stress of two ongoing unsolved cases and still, often, the loss of her husband, it felt as if she were teetering on the edge of the sanity cliff. Maybe she should see the Bureau's shrink again. She groaned inwardly. He'd just want to get into the emotional nitty-gritty. No. She was just lonely. Her body and soul were craving male companionship, parts of her that hadn't accepted that Josh was gone and was never coming back.

Ryan's voice slashed through her thoughts. "Ready to go?"

She looked at him. His forehead shone with sweat. He hated press conferences as much as she did.

She eyed the crowd and forced a smile. "Not really. But, yeah."

Before leaving Omicron, they'd questioned Jason Williams about his relationship with Nicole Henderson. They'd learned Jason and Nicole had become good friends after spending hundreds of hours working together on *The Homecoming*. Victory had also discovered Jason had been in a relationship with the same man for six years. Victory doubted he was the father of Nicole's child and she was reasonably sure a DNA test would confirm that fact. The Wrapper investigation had hit another dead end. Hopefully, the press conference would generate some much-needed new leads. One solid lead. That's all she needed to get onto the killer's trail.

Angie stepped up to the podium. "Can I have your attention, please? We're ready to begin."

Every hetero male eye in the room was transfixed by the shapely blonde. The crowd obeyed and took their seats. Once the room quieted, she gave Victory a nod.

Victory forced her feet to move and headed to the podium, determined not to make eye contact with Melissa Mann. Her squad supervisor, Curtis Stafford followed, and Ryan brought up the rear.

Microphones rose.

She sucked in an unsteady breath, and then let it out. "Good afternoon. For those who don't know me, I'm Agent Victory McClane. M-C-C-L-A-N-E, case-agent-in-charge of The Wrapper investigation. To my right, are Agent Ryan Slater, and Squad Supervisor Curtis Stafford."

Camera shutters clicked, and bulbs flashed.

After a brief pause, she continued. "Early this morning, our office received a call from the Cincinnati Homicide Unit regarding the body of a young woman found in Daniel Drake Park. The victim has been identified as Nicole Lorene Henderson, age twenty-four, of Cincinnati." Victory held up a picture of the young woman—the same photograph, minus the wooden frame, that Lorene Henderson had brought to the coroner's office. "If anyone has any information regarding Ms. Henderson's whereabouts within the forty-eight hours prior, please contact us immediately." This was the part she hated the most, not knowing what the media had in store for her. "I'll answer a couple of brief questions now."

Camera flashes continued to go off.

Melissa's hand shot up first. Victory pretended she

didn't see her and signaled to an unfamiliar male reporter.

He stood.

Victory noticed his press badge dangling around his neck: WKKP TV.

"Is it The Wrapper? Could you elaborate more on the killer's profile and how he chooses his victims?"

"I want to make it clear. We're considering whether the murder of Ms. Henderson is related to those of other young women over the past decade. The evidence suggests it could be the same perpetrator. Our original profile has not changed. A single white male, twenty-five to forty, at least six feet tall, and in good physical shape. Regarding the second part of your question, some serial murderers often select their victims based on physical or personal traits, only victimizing those who fit their mold." She picked up the glass of water next to her and took a drink. "Next question."

To her left, in the front row, she nodded to Marshall Hines, a veteran reporter for the *Cincinnati Enquirer*. He was scribbling something on a small notepad.

"Does the FBI have a theory as to why The Wrapper dumps his victims in a park?"

"Again, I want to make it very clear I'm speaking in general terms only." Her voice was steady and confident, but her stomach was twisting in knots. "Generally, most serial murderers already have an idea where they want to dispose of their victims' remains, choosing a locale that best suits their needs. Usually, a remote or secluded setting, a place significant to them. One last question."

Another reporter caught Victory's attention. She was a young, green-eyed, petite brunette. The Wrapper's ideal victim.

"Do you have *any* leads?" The reporter's voice quivered as she spoke.

They had nothing. Victory felt a stab of anger and guilt. Not a single workable lead and she wasn't going to reveal that fact. They'd eat her alive. "Not anything we can share at this time. We'll keep you updated."

Victory stepped back and started heading for the door. Ryan and Curtis followed.

Melissa Mann bounced to her feet and hurled questions in their direction. "Isn't it true Nicole Henderson was pregnant? Aren't you worried the killer may now be hunting pregnant women, Agent McClane?"

Victory froze in mid-step.

The crowd gasped. Shutters clicked and clicked...

Public knowledge of Nicole's pregnancy was the last thing Victory expected to hear. Anger boiled inside her. Shit like this shouldn't happen. Disgusted, Victory left the conference room as someone yelled, "What about Eddie Bullington's death? Why is the FBI involved?"

In the hallway, away from the commotion, her squad supervisor's round face was tight and red. A look Victory had seen many times. Curtis was mad as hell.

His eyes narrowed. "I want to know how the hell she found out about the pregnancy. It better not have been leaked from this office."

"I can pretty much guarantee it wasn't. Mann has someone inside the coroner's office feeding her information. I'm sure that's it." Ryan shook his head. "I wonder how much she paid for that tidbit."

The thought made Victory's insides roll.

"No more media updates unless necessary." Curtis looked at Victory, his face still flaming red.

"Yes, sir." If Victory had her way, she would never

have another press conference again. Her squad supervisor swiped his hand across his now perspiring forehead. "I've got to get back and look after this fire before shit hits the fan."

Victory didn't notice Curtis leave because she too was busy watching Melissa enter the women's washroom, alone.

A shit storm of her own was about to hit. Victory turned to Ryan. "I'll meet you upstairs."

"Behave yourself, Vic."

"Not this time."

She rushed down the hallway. Inside the washroom, Victory yanked a metal trash can across the linoleum floor and shoved it in front of the door to stop anyone from entering. This was between her and the reporter. No one else.

Melissa was standing in front of the mirror, fluffing her bleached blonde hair. Her blue eyes widened in surprise. "What the hell are you doing?"

Anger flooded Victory's veins. "That was totally irresponsible. Don't you have any consideration for Nicole Henderson's family? And you may have just put more women in danger."

"Her pregnancy is news, Agent McClane." Melissa pouted and checked her hot pink lipstick in the mirror. "You know how it works."

Victory gritted her teeth. Frustration and the lack of sleep kicked in full force. "Listen, you arrogant, ego-tripping little shark." Her hands balled into fists at her sides and it took every ounce of willpower not to pop the reporter in the mouth. "You don't care who you hurt. Just like when you threw me under the bus last year, blaming my husband's death on me because I had to stop at the bank. Frank Sanders killed Josh. Not me. Get your damn facts straight."

Biting back tears, Victory spun around out of Melissa's view. The reporter was not going to see her cry. Not a chance. Victory booted the trash can out of the way. Garbage spewed across the floor. She flung the washroom door open and marched down the hallway.

"Wait, Agent McClane." Melissa hurried behind her. "I'm just trying to do my job. I have some information about Eddie Bullington's death. It's important."

❈   ❈   ❈

After leaving the field office, Victory sped down US-50, frustrated she'd allowed Melissa to get to her. Rush-hour headlights and taillights made the wet highway shimmer like ice. Windshield wipers flapped and squeaked, fighting to keep up with the heavy wet snow. She eyed the speedometer and realized she was driving almost twenty miles over the speed limit. A voice inside her told her to slow down, but anger surged through her and made it almost impossible.

A pickup truck merged into the lane ahead of her.

Victory pumped the brake just in time before she almost rear-ended the truck. Tears fell, obscuring her vision. She pulled to the side of the road and let it all out.

Sunshine poked through the early afternoon clouds and glistened against the neighborhood's snow-covered front lawns. Victory sat in the driver's seat of the family's Honda Odyssey outside their red brick bungalow and punched the horn several times, her gaze trained on the front door.

Jade emerged, carrying a banker's box. A large stuffed elephant was tucked under her arm.

She walked past the driver's window. "God, Mom. You just can't wait to get rid of me again, can you?"

"You found me out. Now hurry up and get in. Where's your father?"

Victory hit the horn again.

"Why on earth do you need to bring Fanny? You haven't even looked at her in years."

Victory watched in the rear-view mirror, growing more impatient, as Jade stuffed the animal between some boxes and crawled over the seat to the middle of the second row. "I didn't have to look at her. I always knew she was there for me."

"I'm sure your roommate will be impressed, seeing that monstrosity coming down the hall."

"Don't call Fanny a monstrosity! What's wrong with you?"

Victory's gaze traveled back to the house. "Your dad is what's wrong with me." *She poked her head out the window.* "C'mon, Josh!"

Josh stepped out the door, keys in hand. He balanced a box on his knee as he tried to lock the front door.

"Look at him." *Victory shook her head.* "He won't take the five seconds to set the box down because he doesn't want to waste time, and his juggling act will end up costing him five minutes."

Josh locked the door, smiled smugly, and made his way to the passenger seat after putting the box into the back.

Victory threw the vehicle into reverse and zoomed out of the driveway. "Well, thank you, sir, for gracing us with your eventual presence."

Josh smiled and peered over his shoulder at Jade. "Remind me who chose to work on her day off instead of getting you back to college this morning? We still have a four-hour drive ahead of us."

"Umm, I think it was...Oh, that was...Mom."

"You're right. It was." Josh smirked. "Funny, it seems to be the same Mom who's blaming us for being late now."

"The very same one," Jade said.

"Yeah well, you guys go out and catch bad guys to keep the world safe then." Victory slapped the steering wheel. "Oh shit."

Josh's eyebrows raised. "Shit, what?"

"The insurance reimbursement. I forgot to deposit it yesterday.

"So? Do it tonight, or tomorrow morning."

"It needs to be in before the end of the day. Today. The mortgage payment will bounce otherwise."

Jade let out a long sigh. "Great planning, Mom. Now I'm going to be late for the biggest campus party of the season."

"Be quiet, you. The ATM at First National is the closest. It won't take long." Victory flicked on the turning signal and turned left.

*　　*　　*

Fifteen minutes later, Victory steered into the busy parking lot of the First National bank and put the vehicle in park. She dug through her purse and held up the check. "I'll just be a second. Back in two shakes of a lamb's tail." She smiled and placed her hand on the door's release ready to get out.

"What does that even mean, Mom?"

"It means I'll be quick."

"I know, but I—oh shit."

Victory turned and looked at her daughter. "Shit, what?"

"Contact lens cleaner."

"What about it?"

"I'm all out. Gotta get some. Like, now."

Victory glanced at her husband and sighed.

Josh pointed across and up the busy street, then snatched the check from Victory's hand. "There's a Walgreen's up the block. Run her over, and I'll toss this in the account." He opened the door and hopped out.

Victory nodded, then sped out of the lot, toward the drug store.

❊   ❊   ❊

While she waited for Jade to make her purchase, which seemed to be taking forever, Victory turned up the volume on the radio. She tapped her fingers on the steering wheel and half-hummed, half-sang along with Fleetwood Mac's "Don't Stop". When the song was done, she shut off the radio and opened the window a few inches. Freezing air seeped inside.

In the distance, sirens howled. Her eyes shifted to the side mirror. A stream of police vehicles, lights flashing, sirens shrieking, sped toward the bank. Her heart stopped. Josh!

Victory flung the door open and jumped out. Her boots pounded the street as she darted through traffic, almost getting hit by vehicles more than once. Tires squealed, horns blasted.

She sprinted around the corner, her chest heaving. Officers had cordoned off the area with police tape. Her heart pounded. Dozens of police vehicles, ambulances, and a SWAT van blocked the sidewalk in front of a crowd of onlookers gathered at the bank.

Victory elbowed through the jostling mob and ducked under the police tape. She spotted FBI SWAT Commander Matt Harris. She raced to him. "Matt! Where's Josh? Where is he,

Matt? What's going on?"

His eyes drifted to the bank. His expression turned grim. "Victory, the shooter's down but...it's not good."

She sidestepped him.

Matt grabbed her arm to try to stop her. "Wait, Victory."

She shook free and ran.

❋   ❋   ❋

Victory stopped dead inside the bank's double doors, her legs frozen. Holiday music churned a jolly tune from the bank's speakers. A police officer walked past her carrying a crying little girl. Her pink winter coat was spattered and stained with dark red blood. Two SWAT members were busy ushering a group of horrified customers and employees past her and out of the bank.

Victory scanned each face. Josh wasn't with them. Panic set in. She looked away and took a few shaky steps.

In front of her, a body. His face was covered with a black ski mask. A few feet away, a woman with brown hair was flat on her back, arms sprawled out at her sides with a gaping bullet wound at the top of her head. To the right of the woman, a young man, a bank employee, his plastic ID still pinned to his striped shirt. His lifeless body was propped up against the bottom of the bank counter. Dead blue eyes stared back, wide.

Victory's eyes darted to a Christmas tree in the corner. Then she spotted him. His boots...his shirt. So much blood.

She couldn't breathe. Her legs buckled, and the world slipped away. Victory dropped to her knees and wailed.

❋   ❋   ❋

At six-fifteen, Victory arrived home, exhausted and

emotionally drained. After a brief conversation in the elevator with Suzanne, a lawyer who lived below her, Victory unlocked her apartment door on the twenty-ninth floor. She turned the light on and dead-bolted the door behind her. She hated coming home. Hated the silence.

The Radcliffe Towers offered lots of perks including a twenty-four-hour fitness center, pool, spa, and a rooftop deck. The building was convenient, only a twenty-five-minute drive to the field office. Many summer evenings she had sat on the deck enjoying a beer, taking in the spectacular city skyline. But it wasn't home. Victory glanced at the cream-colored leather sofa and chair, coffee tables with shiny metal legs, and the rich cherry-colored bamboo floors. No matter how much time or money she spent on decorating, the apartment never felt like home.

She missed her house in Cleveland, a cozy four-bedroom brick bungalow that she and Josh had bought right after she'd graduated from the Academy. Her stomach clenched. It wasn't the actual structure Victory missed. It was what the home had meant to her, Josh, and Jade. Love. Safety. Happiness. The way Victory thought the rest of her life would be. Victory wriggled out of her coat and let it drop onto the arm of the couch. As she took off her boots, the apartment intercom buzzed, forcing her melancholy mood on hold. She checked the viewer screen to see Agent Tom Mendez, a tall, and attractive Latino with boyish good looks. He had a white file folder in his hand.

"C'mon up, Tom." Victory hit the button to let him in.

She turned and stared at the mess on the coffee

table, then quickly gathered the newspapers, books, file folders, and stacked them in a neater pile on the table.

Minutes later she opened the door. "Hey, thanks for stopping by. It's been a crazy day, a really long one. I was hoping to meet with you at the office but obviously, that didn't pan out."

He shot her a smile. "Hey, no worries."

"Want a beer or something?"

He shook his head. "No, thanks. Can't stay long, but here's the file on Bullington's hate crime investigation. Can't say I'm surprised he's dead." He handed her the folder.

It was sad no one seemed shocked by the radio host's death. Not the FBI. Not even the victim's sister.

"What's the status of your investigation?"

"It went south a while ago. I had forwarded everything to the Civil Rights Division at the Department of Justice. Not enough evidence. The file was closed about a month ago."

"Was Bullington notified?"

"Yup. Spoke with him in person. The guy was scared to death. So much so, that the radio station had forked out a large amount of dough to hire a bodyguard through a private security firm," Tom said.

"What was his name?"

"The bodyguard? Wilson. Tyler Wilson. There's half a page on him in there. If one thing's clear, it's that the station didn't want anything to happen to their money-maker. Bullington had also mentioned they were installing the best home security system money could buy."

"Well, he definitely did that. Not that it helped." This was the first Victory had heard about a bodyguard. She made a mental note to check into the guy. "Exactly how was Bullington threatened?"

He leaned against the wall. "Someone left a blood-splattered letter tacked to his front door, along with a cloth armband. Official NSM garb. White with red circles and a black swastika. The note went into graphic detail about chopping him up into little pieces if he ever did another negative radio show about them or neo-Nazi groups in general."

Victory leafed through the contents of the folder. "But the guy wasn't cut up. He took a bullet in the head. A homicide with a half-assed attempt to make it look like a suicide, it seems."

"Yeah, that's interesting. Maybe they offed him to take the heat off the group after the letter incident."

Victory doubted the racist group had anything to do with the radio host's death. A coincidental threat and nothing more, but, like every other seemingly-unrelated bit of information, it would need to be checked out. "Any suspects at the time?"

"No one specific. But one name kept popping up. Michael Vertus, a white supremacist, and troublemaker from way back. Two years ago, he was a lieutenant with the Ohio chapter. Now he runs a rogue online group called *Whites Rise-Up dot com*, a typical neo-Nazi propaganda site. With these guys, hatred and intimidation is the name of the game. I heard he was hanging low in Cleveland, with his sister on the family farm."

Victory's breath came fast and uneven. Cleveland. The last place she wanted to go. Her gaze traveled to the mantel to the wedding photograph of her and Josh.

"Any thoughts on that one yet?" Tom asked.

"Crime scene kind of points to The Shadow. But we'll be checking out Vertus regardless."

"The Shadow? I've overheard some solemn whispers about that one over the years. A story that mommy and daddy FBI agents use to scare their kids. Totally unexplainable stuff. You think there might be something there?"

"Just a hunch. But if it is him, a radio personality is a slightly different target for him. That deviation that could help nail him."

"If you try to nail him, he'd probably just evaporate or something."

Victory laughed. "You might not be too far off on that."

"Well, gotta go and get my youngest from karate class. Best of luck with both cases, Victory." He glanced at the folder then back to her. "Let me know if you need anything else on Bullington."

"I will. And thanks again, Tom."

After he left, Victory locked the door and headed into the kitchen. She grabbed a bottle of beer and a plate of two-day-old pasta from the fridge, then sat at the kitchen table and picked at the food. Her thoughts danced from one possibility to another. Was Michael Vertus, The Shadow? What about the bodyguard? Was he involved? Too many questions and not enough answers. She decided to give Ryan a quick call to let him know what she'd learned.

"Hey, Vic. What's up?"

She heard Angie's bubbly voice muffled in the background. Victory didn't care if the two were seeing each other as long as their relationship didn't affect their work. Their boss, on the other hand, wouldn't be happy. He had an old-school FBI attitude. Agents were men of action, poster boys for J. Edgar Hoover's G-Men, and didn't need a woman distracting them from catching the bad guys, despite Hoover's private penchant for wearing pretty dresses. As much as Victory hated to admit it, at times, it was still very much a man's world.

"Got a possible lead in the Bullington case we need to look into." Victory told Ryan about Michael Vertus and the bodyguard.

"It's worth checking out."

"Pick me up in the morning. I want to get an early start. And grab me an extra-large coffee. I'm going to need it." Victory heard Angie's voice again. It sounded as if the two were having fun and it made her miss her husband even more.

"Okay, see you in the morning."

She placed the phone down and glanced around the empty kitchen, her gloomy mood resurfacing.

She had met Josh, a forensic dentist, while he was working with the medical examiner's office in Cleveland after what was suspected of being The Shadow's first kill. Ryan had introduced them, and it was love at first sight. Six months later they were married. Victory twisted her white gold wedding band and her heart squeezed at the lifetime of memories of their lives together she had locked away, terrified they would one day disappear. She took another drink of her beer and glanced at the accordion file folder at the end of the table.

Some cases never left her. The Shadow case was one of them. She and Ryan had spent thousands of hours working the case. Decades later, they were still no closer to coming up with a single suspect.

Victory didn't want to contact Melissa Mann, but after learning more about Eddie Bullington, she wanted to know what information the reporter was sitting on.

Her stomach churned. She picked up the phone and called the reporter. After seven rings, the call went to voicemail.

"This is Melissa Mann. Got something for me? Leave it here and I'll get back to you as soon as I can."

A long beep. Silence.

Victory hesitated for a moment. "It's Victory McClane. Let's talk tomorrow afternoon." She disconnected, hoping she wasn't going to regret contacting the woman.

A sudden knock at the door startled her.

Victory got up and went and answered the door. It was John, the building's doorman, clutching a large cranberry red vase, containing at least three dozen long-stemmed white Peruvian lilies. She stared at the flowers, baffled as to who could have sent them.

"They sure are mighty pretty. It looks like you made a lasting impression on someone, Mrs. McClane."

"I—guess so." She fought to keep the mention of *Mrs* from sending her reeling back into the past.

He passed her the bouquet and grinned. "Have a good night, Ma'am."

Victory gave him a small smile. "Thanks. You too, John." She shoved the door closed with her foot and used the palm of her free hand to secure the lock. After placing the vase on the kitchen table, she found a small white envelope hidden within the stems. She opened it and read the card:

Have dinner with me
Derrick
513-421-5698

Her pulse sped up. How did he know lilies were her

favorite, a detail only Josh and Jade were aware of? How did he know where she lived? It wasn't as if her address was listed anywhere, and there was no way anyone at the Bureau would have given out her personal information. The more she thought about it, the more suspicious she became. Had he followed her home? He definitely had her attention. She stared at the flowers. If Derrick Lynn wanted to play, Victory was up to the challenge. It was as if he was trying too hard and she knew from years of experience that fact alone was a huge red flag.

CHAPTER EIGHT

Inside the living room of his Fairfield Avenue home overlooking the Ohio River, Derrick poured two double shots of scotch, an expensive thirty-five-year-old sweet toffee and fruit blend, his father's favorite.

"It's good to see you, son."

He hadn't seen his father since last summer and couldn't remember the last time they'd had dinner or even a drink together.

His father, Roland, was a tall and regal-looking man with the same dark hair as Derrick with a splash of gray at his temples, cut in a longer than usual military-style buzz cut. He was dressed impeccably in his usual Washington attire; a black suit, crisp white shirt, and a black and red pinstriped tie.

"Good to see you too. The palace intrigue keeping you busy back in D.C.?" Derrick handed him a drink and sat across from him in one of the modern wingback chairs.

"As long as there's a thirst for political power, my kind will never be unemployed. Nor will yours, son." Roland took a drink of his scotch. "I've been reading that your business is doing quite well, considering it was supposed to be just a front in the first place. I'm proud of you."

"Come on, Dad. You didn't make an eight-hour drive to tell me you're proud of me."

Roland set his glass on the coffee table. "No. It's related to the previous task."

"Another loudmouth blowhard on the radio?"

His eyes shifted to the window then back to Derrick. "Any problems with Bullington?"

Derrick's thoughts jumped to Victory. He wasn't going to tell his father about his little slip with the FBI agent. He knew the man wouldn't approve. "Everything went smoothly."

His father leaned forward, rested his elbows on his knees, and clasped his hands together. "Do you know why Bullington became a task, Derrick?"

"Nope, and I don't want to. It's not in my job description."

"He found out about the Elara Project."

"You're kidding. How? And how did he keep his mouth shut about it?"

"He had every intention of exposing us, waiting for the most opportune moment to get the most bang for his buck. He planned on doing a live show next week."

"Let me guess. During the president's visit on infrastructure."

Roland nodded. "That's when he was going to unleash his expose—he and his source.

"Who's the source?"

"A television reporter."

Derrick downed his drink, got up, and went to pour another. "But we control the networks and what can be reported about us. That's never been an issue."

"She's not from a network. Keeping her in line hasn't been an option, not without admitting the project is indeed real."

Derrick glanced over his shoulder. "Who's her source?"

"Your immediate concern should be—who is *she*?"

"Alright." Derrick sat back down, clutching his drink.

"Melissa Mann. She works for a local TV station—"

"I know who she is."

Roland leaned back in the chair. "She needs to be stopped. She'll be quite frightened after hearing about Bullington's death."

"She could snap and start talking right away."

"Or…she could protect the information in the event of her untimely death. The woman isn't stupid."

"You know the deal, Dad. No women.

"Would you rather have the whole house of cards come toppling down? On top of you? On top of us?"

Growing up, he remembered his father telling him about a female government official he had taken care of in the early '80s for the sake of national security. "I'm not the only one who can perform the task. You could do it."

His father's jaw tightened, and his eyes hardened. "This is not a request, son. Comes directly from the top. The last thing we need is a category four shit storm. Shelter from the storm. That's what you must provide for us."

A few beats of tense silence passed between the men.

Roland downed his drink, then checked his Jaeger-LeCoultre watch. "I need to get back."

Derrick could tell this side trip had cost his father a great deal of valuable time. As they walked to the front of the house, a tight knot formed in the pit of Derrick's stomach. He didn't like feeling stuck with no options. But protecting the Elara Project was the only thing that mattered. He didn't have a choice. He opened the front door. Chilly air tunneled inside. At the same time as his father stepped outside, the three black Secret Service Suburbans in the driveway fired up. Headlights flicked on simultaneously.

Roland's eyes narrowed. "Don't ever forget what you are, son—who you serve." He handed Derrick a piece of paper with an address written on it. "Let me know as soon as the task is done."

His father's voice was icy, hard. Derrick reluctantly took the paper and watched the man climb into the back of one of the vehicles. A few seconds later, the vehicles backed out of the driveway and paraded up the street.

Victory watched the morning sun slowly poke through the slate-colored clouds. At ten o'clock she was still tired and worn out from yesterday's long hours. Despite exhaustion, sleep hadn't come easily. Melissa Mann still hadn't returned her call. Victory suspected the reporter was giving her the runaround.

"Are you going to be okay?" Ryan asked. "I know this isn't the easiest thing for you, coming back to Cleveland."

No, she wasn't okay, but she didn't have a choice. "I have to be."

At some point, Victory knew she'd be returning to Cleveland regardless of how she felt. She pushed down the guilt and anxiety, knowing she could never escape the past. Part of her wanted to drive by her old house to see what the place looked like now. It was too soon. She'd fall apart. She needed to focus on her job because it was the only thing keeping her together.

In the distance, open snow-covered rolling hills came into view. They were entering farm country. Light snow danced in the air and twinkled in the sunlight like glitter.

Victory glanced at Ryan. "Guess who sent me flowers?"

Ryan shrugged. "Hermes?"

"Derrick Lynn."

Ryan's eyebrows raised. "What? How the hell did he know where you live?"

"It's a mystery, like all the other mysteries we're dealing with right now."

"I'm not liking this, Vic. Kinda creepy."

"Don't worry, I'm on it." She turned down the heat and cracked open the window an inch or so. "The farm should be coming up soon."

Unsure of how Michael Vertus would react to their arrival, Victory wasn't taking any chances. She'd witnessed first-hand what white supremacist members could do from church shootings to bombing a Sikh temple. "We go in hot. Vests and 12 gauges."

Ryan slowed the SUV and turned right onto the bumpy road, leading to the property as Victory's phone rang. She snatched the phone from her jacket pocket. "McClane."

"Hey Vic, it's Sean. I had a chat with Bullington's bodyguard. He's not the guy we're looking for. Tyler Wilson isn't The Shadow. He said he followed Bullington home as usual and made sure he was inside before he left for his next security gig. He was meeting a corporate suit at the airport. His story checks out."

She wasn't surprised. "I doubt Michael Vertus is involved either. I'll let you know if we learn anything new. We're just pulling up to the farmhouse now."

"Stay safe. You never know with those wing-nuts."

"We will."

Ryan steered the vehicle to the side of the road and parked under a row of trees about five hundred yards from the main house. He shut the engine off and scrubbed his hand over his face. "Brody?"

Victory nodded and opened the door. "We can rule out the bodyguard."

"I figured as much." Ryan opened the door and got out. "Looks like our friend has company."

She spotted five men, including Michael Vertus, smoking and talking on a shabby wooden front porch of the dilapidated two-storey brick house. All the men were wearing heavy red and black checked flannel jackets. Their heads were shaved, marked with various tattoos and swastikas.

Ryan opened the back of the SUV, folded back the seat, and unlocked the compartment containing their ballistic vests and Remington 870 shotguns.

Victory removed her winter coat and tossed it in the vehicle. A chill skated across her skin, the wind cutting through her thick sweater. After securing her vest, she grabbed one of the shotguns, pressed the safety switch forward, pulled back the pump slide, and placed a 12-gauge shell against the loading port. She pushed a shell inside and forward, then repeated the action until all the shells were loaded. She grabbed her phone from her coat and shoved it into the back pocket of her pants.

Ryan finished loading his weapon and peered over

the roof of the vehicle. "Not too thrilled about being out-numbered if this goes south. You never know how many weapons these assholes have stockpiled on the prop-erty."

Victory wasn't thrilled either. There wasn't much cover on the way up to the house, and the last thing they needed was a shootout. Victory held the shotgun a little tighter than normal, preparing herself for the worst.

As they plodded side-by-side up the driveway, crisp snow crunched and squealed under the rubber soles of their boots. Two make-shift signs made from wooden slabs crudely painted with red spray paint were ham-mered to tree trunks. One said, NO TRESPASSING, the other, WHITES ONLY. Victory kept the shotgun pointed toward the ground and her eyes glued to the men, search-ing for any indication things could turn nasty.

Michael Vertus, a tall beanpole of a man with a crooked nose spotted them first. He was well-known to the local cops and had a long record, including numer-ous weapons and assault charges. He sauntered down the front steps and stopped on the last one. The other men clustered around him like groupies.

Vertus laughed like a manic. "Well, what have we got here?"

"Keep an eye on the short one," Ryan said to her quietly. "He's too fidgety."

Victory's pulse sped up. The short one might have been height-limited, but he had a thick neck and was bulked unnaturally with muscle. She stopped and planted her feet firmly on the ground in case she needed to use the weapon. Her eyes shifted back and forth to each man. "We just want to talk to you, Vertus."

"You're trespassing." He shot her a cocky grin. "Can't

you pigs read the signs?"

"Tell them to get the hell out of here," the shortest man of the group said, as he flicked his cigarette butt over the porch railing.

Ryan raised his shotgun a few inches higher as a show of force.

Victory followed his lead, then took a few more steps and stopped again. "We aren't leaving until we talk to you. We can do this the easy way—or I can have two dozen cops here in an instant. You don't want that to happen because the odds won't be in your favor. Actually, they aren't in your favor right now."

Vertus looked at her with a confused expression on his face. "Odds?"

"Do you want the ATF here searching the property? I'm guessing not."

The smug grin on his face immediately disappeared. He strutted toward them with his arms at his side.

Victory raised the gun and aimed the barrel evenly at his chest. "That's close enough."

Ryan moved to the right of her and trained his shotgun on the others. "Tell your friends to beat it."

A few seconds went by before Vertus peered over his shoulder and nodded to his men.

They headed to a beat-up black Chevy Blazer parked next to the house. Short-man had a set of keys dangling in his hand. He opened the driver side door and glared at Victory with stormy brown eyes, while the others walked to the other side of the vehicle.

Victory had an uneasy feeling in the pit of her stomach. Her eyes darted to Vertus and then back to Short-man. He reached into his jacket pocket and started to pull something out.

Her heart pounded double-time. She spotted the glint of shiny metal. Victory fired.

The slug slammed into the back window of the Blazer, punching a hole the size of a large grapefruit. Glass exploded. Chunks showered the trunk and into the back seat.

She yanked the pump slide back and prepared to shoot again. "Drop the gun."

"Do what she says," Vertus yelled. "We don't need any more trouble."

She gripped the weapon tighter. "Listen to him. At least the light bulb is partially on." She aimed the barrel of the shotgun at Short-man's leg. "You may want to keep that leg."

The man's eyes narrowed and held a steely determination. Finally, he chucked the weapon in the snow.

Ryan cautiously stepped toward the men. "Everyone up against the Blazer. Keep your hands where we can see them." After he searched each one, he found two more weapons and confiscated them. "Get the hell out of here, you damn fools."

Victory exhaled, realizing she had been holding her breath. They were fools, lucky she hadn't arrested them.

The Blazer did a three-sixty, snow spitting out under the tires, like a snowblower stuck in high gear, firing snow in every direction. The vehicle blasted past her and off the property.

Ryan came up behind Vertus, yanked his hands behind him, and handcuffed him. He did a body search and discovered a gun tucked in the back waistband of the man's jeans. He threw it on the ground.

Victory lowered the shotgun. Her eyes traveled to Vertus' gun. "Beanpole. You've got a lot of explaining to do." Then her phone rang. "Take him inside." Clutching the shotgun under her arm, she awkwardly extracted the phone from her pocket. "What's up, Sean?"

"Vic, you and Ryan need to get back here. We've got a missing girl."

Victory lowered the phone and imagined the worst, as she watched Ryan shove Michael Vertus toward the house.

❋　❋　❋

Inside his office at the Pentagon, Roland picked up his phone from his desk and punched in the set of numbers.

After three rings, the voice on the other end said, "I was expecting your call."

"I spoke with Derrick earlier," Roland said.

"I hope you have good news."

"He was reluctant. But I drove the message home. He knows he doesn't have a choice. He was reminded who he works for. I'm confident the issue will be taken care of in a timely manner."

"I'm sure it's difficult for him, but he knows what he signed up for years ago. Sometimes sacrifices need to be made to protect others. In this case—all of us, and the project."

There was a short pause on the other end. "We're at war on many various levels. This is one of those times. The Elara Project *must* remain buried at any cost."

❋　❋　❋

He wondered how long this one would scream before she passed out from the pain. She had to be punished, like the rest. She looked so much like Lily, the resemblance uncanny. The thought of his ex-fiancé made every muscle in his body tight and hard and crawl with hatred. He couldn't find her, and not from the lack of trying. He'd searched for years after she'd disappeared, leaving him for another man a week before their wedding.

No one walked away from him.

Inside the barren warehouse, he stared at the woman dressed only in panties and a bra wrapped in bubble wrap, bound to a metal kitchen chair with a thick steel cable. For now, this one would have to do until he found Lily.

She was a pretty, petite, twenty-three-year-old he'd met the night before at a dance club on the other side of town. She was more than willing to go home with him, where he had kept her drugged before transporting her to the warehouse.

He was happy with his choice. Long brown hair hung over her breasts, and wide green eyes stared at him with fear and dazed awareness. She knew she was going to die.

With a gloved hand, he gently moved greasy strands of hair from her slick forehead and inhaled the sweet scent of the baby oil he had doused her body with earlier.

The woman flinched at his touch. Bubble wrap popped.

Poor thing. If she only knew what was about to happen. He bent and whispered in her ear. "It's okay." Soon, the duct tape from her mouth. He couldn't wait.

Her eyes bulged, bug-like. Tears streamed down her oily cheeks.

He double-checked the four space heaters encircling the woman, each set less than a foot from her body, positioned at different heights, and he thought about the nickname the FBI had given him, *The Wrapper*.

He booted one of the thick extension cords aside. He had watched the FBI's news conference earlier. What a joke. Agent McClane made him sound like a fucking rapper on MTV. At least they'd labeled Jeffrey Dahmer, *The Milwaukee Cannibal*, and Posteal Laskey had earned the name, *The Cincinnati Strangler*. He deserved the same respect. He was Ohio's *Bubble Wrap Killer*. Nothing more. Nothing less. The FBI agent was just angry she couldn't catch him and never would. He laughed, his deep, roaring voice reverberating throughout the destitute space.

He donned a new HazMat suit and stood in front of the woman, smiling. Adrenaline spiked through his veins. With a flick of a handheld switch, all four heaters clicked on and roared to life. Their burners turned fiery red, producing a brilliant glow. Dust particles danced in the light as a horde of rats scurried by, their beady black eyes darting back and forth, sensing the imminent danger.

Within minutes the baby oil would heat, and the bubble wrap would melt into her skin. Oh, the glorious pain he was about to inflict on her. She looked so much like Lily. The woman deserved it.

They all did.

He hesitated for a second, his hands shaking from the adrenaline rush, then ripped the duct tape from her mouth and jumped out of the intense heat. Euphoria flooded his body, a high he felt with each kill.

Shrill screams and begging surrounded him. He tilted his head and watched as her once-stunning features blurred and deformed like a melting wax figure. It didn't take long before her body went limp, as burnt flesh and blood slid from her bones onto the concrete floor.

＊ ＊ ＊

At two-forty-five in the morning, Derrick poured a scotch and stood in front of the living room window, staring at the rainbow of lights, reflecting and shimmering off the river. Guilt twisted through him. He'd made a vow to never harm a woman or a child. He had been forced to take care of the reporter to protect the Elara project and everyone involved. He gulped down his scotch and cursed to himself, angry he'd been put in the position in the first place. No one was supposed to know about the project.

He thought about his childhood and how he had always felt as if he was different. It wasn't until he was thirteen when he realized he wasn't like the other kids at school. His height, pale skin, and dark hair made him an easy target by a group of boys led by Jake Needham.

Every day after school, Jake and his pals would corner him on the way home, harass him, and call him names, saying things like, "If you died no one would care because you already look like you're dead."

Fed up with the constant bullying, Derrick had lost his temper and somehow used his mind to move a large rock, smashing Jake over the head, putting the kid in the hospital for eight weeks with a cracked skull and a severe concussion.

After the incident, Derrick was labeled the bully. A freak. He doubted any of the kids involved understood what had happened that day. At the time, he had no idea either. All he knew was he had applied all his anger and energy at the rock. And it just happened. He could still hear the gruesome hollow crack when the rock smacked the back of Jake's skull. The following day he was expelled from school, never allowed to return.

He grew up without friends, daydreaming of one day owning his own business. Being alone never bothered him. He embraced it and never had to worry that he would hurt anyone else. But everything changed on his twenty-first birthday when his grandfather drove him to a secret location in Fort Meade, Maryland, where he was taught how to use etheric traveling along with his gift of psychokinesis, to become the government's newest lethal weapon. There were others recruited into the program over the years with special abilities that most people would never believe existed.

His thoughts turned to his mother. He tried to see her as often as possible. She was happy and content, married to her high-school sweetheart, and living in D.C. His parents had been divorced for over thirty years. To this day, his mother refused to discuss what had happened. Derrick could only surmise the failure of their relationship was due to his father's decision to put his country first and his family last, which the man had done most of his adult life.

He bent over the laptop keyboard and typed, *"Task completed"*, then ran the DoD's encryption software. With the message encoded for his father's eyes only, he sent the email. A minute passed. A ding. A message box filled the screen.

Contact needs to meet - 2 pm

Derrick stared at the message. From previous meetings with their contact, a helicopter had been booked at the airfield on Taylor Road. He downed the rest of his drink and set the glass on the coffee table, harder than usual, still angry about the task that had been forced upon him.

* * *

After hearing the woman take her last breath, the man moved the body onto a large piece of thick plastic and rolled it up like a carpet. As he secured the plastic with duct tape, he scolded himself for the split-second flicker of guilt he felt for what he had done. The guilt passed quickly. It always did. He lifted the body and placed it in the trunk of his car. Sweat ran down the sides of his face. She was much heavier than he had anticipated. Dead weight usually was. He studied the body one last time. Chipped remnants of the hot pink nail polish left on three of her fingernails glistened neon bright against her blackened flesh.

She had the same round face and angelic features as his Lily. He would find her one day and, when he did, she would suffer a hundred times worse than the look-a-likes. That day was coming. Suddenly the latex gloves felt tight and claustrophobic. He stripped them off and shoved them into his sweatshirt pocket, then slammed the trunk closed. He unzipped the HazMat suit and took it off, leaving it, the booties, and the gloves in a heap on the floor. He'd return to clean up and destroy any evidence after he dumped the body.

He climbed into his car parked inside the loading bay and twisted the key in the ignition. The engine roared to life inside the echoing confines of the warehouse walls. A pungent stench floated from the trunk, a nauseating mix of bodily fluids, burnt meat, and exhaust fumes. The smell clung inside of his nostrils and coated his tongue. He had already put a few dabs of vapor rub up his nose earlier to help with the atrocious odor. It wasn't helping. He wound down the window and swallowed hard, fighting back the sour vomit rising in his throat. Frosty night air flooded the interior of the vehicle and made his damp skin prickle. He leaned his head back on the headrest, inhaled through his nose, and exhaled through his mouth until his stomach settled.

It was quiet at three in the morning. While most people were sleeping, he was dreaming of his next kill. He wouldn't stop until he found Lily.

The large industrial area was made up of a maze of warehouses, distribution centers, and a plastics manufacturer. The buildings were old and worn, built in the early 1970s when manufacturing jobs were plentiful. Over the past decade, new businesses had appeared, then disappeared just as quickly.

The spacious warehouse he had rented was hidden deep at the back of the industrial park, away from prying eyes. It was the perfect location and had enough room for his purposes. He steered out of the warehouse, then put the car in park and hopped out. A loud rumble surrounded him. The ground vibrated below his feet as a train sped by to the east of the industrial park, the clatter echoing into the night air.

His greatest dilemma would be deciding which park to use to dump the body. He had already visited seven with his previous victims: four in Cincinnati, and three in Cleveland. He wasn't a risk-taker and wasn't going to take the chance of revisiting any of the sites in case the authorities were watching. He wouldn't put anything past the FBI or Agent McClane. There was always a slight risk he could get caught. She was a smart woman. He was smarter.

After closing the heavy bay door and securing it with two locks, he jumped back into the driver's seat, anticipating what was coming next—dumping the body and knowing he'd gotten away with it again.

CHAPTER NINE

Victory and Ryan arrived back at the Cincinnati FBI office four hours later. Sean met them in the hallway. Phones rang, keyboards clicked, and loud chatter came from inside the bullpen. A headache drilled at Victory's temples. She glanced at Sean. "Who reported her missing?"

"Her father. She didn't come home after a night out with two of her girlfriends. A BOLO was sent out an hour ago."

He handed her a copy of the bulletin with a photograph of the missing woman. "Angel Hogan, twenty-three." Urban search and rescue were already dispatched, as well as the canine unit. They're searching area parks here and in Cleveland as we speak." Ryan eyed the picture. "Pretty girl. Maybe she hooked up with some random guy and not our guy."

"That's wishful thinking." Victory stared at Angel's smiling face, brunette hair, and green eyes. Her stomach twisted, knowing there was a good chance it was already too late. "Where was she last seen, Sean?"

"A dance bar over on Pavilion. The Players Club. According to her friends, she left early because she had to study for an exam. They just assumed she got into a cab and went home. I've got a call into the cab companies to see if they had a pickup at the club, matching her description."

Victory was silent, her mind churning. "She's our second girl who disappeared after visiting a bar. A pattern may be emerging."

"He'll change it up again to throw us off his trail. He always has in the past," Sean said.

"Agreed." She spotted Curtis strutting toward them, his jaw tight, his brows furrowed.

"Where are we on the Bullington case?" Curtis asked. "I'm getting a lot of crap from the higher-ups and the mayor. That crap will eventually trickle down to you three."

"Michael Vertus proved to be useless. He didn't have anything to do with the murder—and his gun was legal. That one is hard to believe. We had to cut him loose." She heard the frustration in her voice. "We've got nothing according to forensics. The Shadow killed Bullington.

Curtis wiped the sweat from his brow. "You sure?"

The trail had gone cold. She glanced at Ryan then back to her squad supervisor. "Yes."

Curtis' gaze bore into hers. "Great. A killer ghost, a girl burnt to death by The Wrapper, and now a missing girl." His eyes shifted to the paper in Victory's hand and his tone hardened. "At least try to find her before it's too late."

It was a tall order and Victory had a gut feeling it wasn't going to end well. "We'll do our best, sir."

He shook his head and headed down the hallway toward the elevators.

Victory sighed. "Sean. Talk to the girls again. See if

there's something they've missed. A guy trying to pick them up, bugging them. Anything. The smallest detail could help us."

Sean shot her a nod. "Sure. I'll check in with you later."

After Sean left, Ryan looked at her. "What are we going to do?"

"You're going to talk to the staff at the club. Check the CCTVs and any other cameras in the area, in case the locals missed something."

"What about you?"

"I've got something fun planned. A chat with Melissa Mann at the TV station."

"She finally got back to you?"

Victory heard a ding, then the clang of elevator doors as they closed. "Nope. And before the crap lands on me and splashes on you, I need to speak with her."

"If she isn't playing you and she knows something."

"Right."

"Maybe I should tag along, play referee, help keep things peaceful."

"I'll be fine. No busting heads today. We've got enough on our plate."

Victory walked away, pulled her phone out of her coat pocket, and tried Melissa's number one last time. When the call immediately went to voice mail she disconnected without leaving a message.

Inside the bullpen, she stopped at Angie's desk. The woman was busy on her computer. "Can you call Melissa Mann at WKRC? Have the call transferred to my desk when you make contact."

"Of course." Angie looked up at her. "I heard about the missing girl. I hope you can find her."

Most of the time the job made it difficult to be positive. With two serial killers on the loose, Victory preferred to be realistic under the circumstances. "I have a feeling that's not too likely."

Angie frowned. "I'll make the call in a sec. Curtis wants an email copy of your report about Cleveland, and he wants it now."

"Dotting his i's and crossing his t's, no doubt." She placed the BOLO down on the center of the desk, her nerves tighter than usual. If The Wrapper had taken the woman, the chances of finding her alive were slim to none.

Victory understood the scrutiny they were under and had been for years. People were scared, impatient, wanting to feel safe again—and wanting it yesterday. The sooner she could deliver the better. And she would. As she walked to her desk, frustration swirled, and her thoughts turned to Derrick. He was hiding something and maybe it was time to take him up on his dinner invitation. It was still bothering her how he found out where she lived. Victory planned on asking. She reached into her pocket and pulled out the card with his phone number written on it. She decided to make the call from her office phone, not comfortable with him knowing her cell number. That is if he didn't already.

After a few rings, Derrick's secretary answered and put her through to his office.

"Agent McClane. What can I do for you?"

"Victory."

"Okay. Victory."

"Thanks for the flowers. We need to talk about that."

"Sure. When and where?"

"Season 51 on Vine. Six o'clock." She figured she

might as well pick one of her favorite eateries, a casual restaurant with a city view, and a great Italian menu. Besides, she could use a decent meal and there wasn't much more she personally could do to help find Angel Hogan. There were at least fifty cops and FBI agents out on the street looking for her.

"Shall I send a car to pick you up?"

"I'll meet you there."

"Are you always this straightforward and official-like?"

"It comes with the job. I'll see you later."

Angie appeared at her desk the moment Victory set down the receiver.

"The station said they have no idea where Melissa is. She could be out on an assignment they don't know about, or maybe working at home on a story."

Victory's stomach tightened, and her head thumped harder. The reporter wasn't going to make it easy for her, and that made her question Melissa's motives even more. She rifled through the desk drawer and found the bottle of Aspirins she kept there for days like this. She popped two into her mouth and downed them dry. "Call the station back and get her home address."

By the time Victory left the office and drove to Melissa's home on Monticello Avenue, it was four-thirty in the afternoon. Thankfully, her headache had finally disappeared. She steered into the driveway and shut off the engine. As much as she didn't want to speak to the woman, she didn't have a choice. If Melissa truly knew something that could help with Bullington's murder investigation, then it would be worth it.

The house was a small gray brick ranch with a large front yard and cement-colored attached garage. A tall tree in the middle of the front lawn was weighted down with snow. There weren't any personal touches that made the home stand out, which was odd considering the reporter's classy fashion flair. The house was simply plain compared to the other homes in the Bellmeadow neighborhood decorated with whimsical Christmas decorations and lights.

Victory swung open the door and climbed out. A cold north wind whipped around the corner of the house and thrashed at the treetops. A chill skittered through her, even though she was wearing a heavy Shaker knit sweater underneath her coat. She headed up the snowy walkway to the front door. After knocking numerous times and no one answered, she went and checked the garage. Peering through the window, she saw Melissa's black Volkswagen Jetta parked inside. She rounded the side of the house, leading to the backyard when her phone rang. She dragged the phone from her pocket and smiled when she checked the display.

"Hey, kiddo."

"Hi, Mom. I can't talk long. I have to get back to studying. My friend, Karen, is going to bring me home for your birthday, so you won't have to come and pick me up. Two more days and you'll be as old as the hills."

"Do you have to be such a smartass?" Victory scanned the empty yard and continued walking to the back door.

"I got that from you and Dad."

Victory smiled again at the mention of Josh. Her daughter was very much like her father. She had the same free-spirit, cool demeanor, and humor.

"I'll be in town by four-thirty. Oh—I have to run."

"Just remember life's not all beer and skittles."

"God, Mom. I'm not even going to ask what that means."

Victory's phone beeped three times indicating an incoming call. "I've got another call, hun. Love you."

"Love you too."

Victory disconnected and tapped the 'answer' button. "Already miss me?"

There was a beat of airy silence on the other end before Ryan spoke, then she heard '90s dance music playing in the background.

"Vic, search and rescue found a body at Rapid Run Park in Price Hill."

The air swooshed out of her lungs. "Angel Hogan."

"I'm guessing—yeah.

"You better contact Sean."

"I'm still downtown at the Players Club. I'll meet you at the park."

She took one last look at the back of the house then rushed to her vehicle. "On my way."

✻ ✻ ✻

After a thirty-minute drive and a two-hour helicopter flight from Cincinnati, Derrick sat in the small waiting area outside the Oval Office and waited for his father. Heels clicked on highly polished floors, the high-traffic corridors bustling with staff, military, and Secret Service agents. He spotted his father speaking with White House Chief of Staff, Adien Clark, a stocky man in his late forties with a face like a sad bulldog. Moments later, his father came into the waiting area.

"Sorry, I'm late, son. I was stuck in a meeting with the Chairman of the Joint Chiefs of Staff."

Derrick stood and glanced at the two Secret Service agents standing like poles on each side of the door to the Oval Office. "I know how busy you are. But why was I summoned?"

"We have a delicate situation."

"I hope it's not like the last situation because—"

"I assure you it isn't."

Intrigued, Derrick followed his father into the Oval Office.

The office was tastefully decorated the same as in the Obama days with striped wallpaper, red drapes, and taupe rug bordered with quotes from Abraham Lincoln, Theodore Roosevelt, Franklin D. Roosevelt, Martin Luther King, Jr, and John F. Kennedy. A Christmas tree was erected next to the south garden window, extravagantly embellished with red balls and gold bows.

Myron Burke was sitting behind the historic Resolute desk, the elegant nineteenth-century desk used by seven previous presidents; the same desk at which President Kennedy had signed Proclamation 3504, authorizing the naval quarantine of Cuba. Each time Derrick set foot inside the office he was in awe of the rich history and artwork. A teleprompter, cameras, and lights were ready for the presidential address, regarding the latest terrorist attack in London that claimed over fifty innocent bystanders at an outdoor market.

The president finished straightening his tie and stood, acknowledging their presence. He glanced at Adien. "Give us a few minutes."

Adien looked at his watch as he headed to the door.

"You're live in eighteen minutes."

After the Chief of Staff left and closed the door behind him, the president held out his hand to Derrick. "Good to see you."

Derrick went and shook his hand. "You too, Mr. President."

"I told your father it's been too long since we last met."

Myron Burke was fifty-six, an attractive man with all-American good looks, and in top physical shape despite the rumors, he was an alcoholic. He had a strong and loyal base of constituents because of his tough stance on terrorism.

"It's been about eight months, sir."

"Far too long. Have a seat." The president smiled and moved to the small table with the crystal decanter and glasses on it and poured a couple of shots of whiskey.

Derrick and his father took a seat on the couch.

Myron held out his glass. "Drink?"

"No, thanks," both men said in unison.

Derrick wondered what he was doing here. He was anxious to know.

The president downed his drink and poured another. "Was our issue taken care of?"

Derrick was confused. He was positive his father would have passed along his email to the president. "Early this morning, sir."

Myron sat behind his desk and took a sip of his drink. "There's another problem. We think the reporter kept notes about the Elara Project on her personal laptop."

"The information she and Eddie Bullington planned on revealing to the world," his father added.

Derrick looked at the president. "Do we know the

original source yet?"

"Not yet. Which will create another problem. We need the laptop before someone realizes she's expired. I'm sure you understand what will happen if the authorities or anyone else get their hands on it before we do."

Jail wasn't in his future. Derrick knew how important it was to keep the Elara Project secret. His ass was on the line too. This was beyond his paranormal skills. He'd have to do it the old-fashioned way, break in and steal it. It was a huge risk but too much was at stake.

"Son, I had someone call the TV station pretending to be Mann. As far as anyone knows she's home sick for a couple of days. That should give you enough time to get the laptop."

Derrick wasn't happy about the turn of events. Again, they weren't giving him a choice. "I'll look after it."

The president smiled. "While you're here, I'd like you to take a trip over to Fort Meade and meet our latest recruit. You'll be impressed. Who would have thought that over the decades there would be more people out there with unusual skills this government could utilize to help keep our country safe? Thank you for your service, Derrick. Your grandfather would be proud, as I'm sure your father is as well."

"Thank you, sir."

"The security of our nation is, and always will be, number one." He held his glass up in the air. "To another three years while I'm in the office and hopefully a second term, God willing." He gulped down the rest of his drink and set the empty glass on the desk. "I'll have a car take you to Fort Meade."

*　*　*

As Victory drove to Rapid Run Park, the sun lowered, and wispy thin clouds transformed into shades of golden pink. To the north, the sky was full of tumultuous dark clouds. Another snow storm was brewing. She had called Derrick's secretary on the way and left a message canceling their dinner plans. A small part of her was disappointed, but she was confused as to why. She shoved the thought aside for now and pulled up slowly to the entrance of the park. A river of lights flashed, coming from dozens of police cruisers, FBI, and search and rescue vehicles.

She rolled down the window and showed her ID to one of the officers guarding the entrance. He gave it a long once over with a critical eye and finally let her pass. She steered into the parking lot and found an empty spot next to one of the white ERT vehicles. Victory shut off the engine and watched two uniformed officers blocking off the perimeter with white and blue crime scene police tape. She stayed put for a few minutes, mentally preparing herself for what she'd find at the scene.

A dozen news trucks were parked along the perimeter. Reporters pushed and shoved each other, volleying for a front-seat view. Victory didn't see Melissa Mann. The reporter was probably hiding behind a tree, ready to attack. Victory noticed Curtis and Joe Mains busy talking with reporters. She let out a long sigh and got out of the car.

Ryan met her. Lines etched his forehead. He looked frustrated.

"What's the dynamic-duo up to?" Victory asked.

"They're calming the public."

"The word calming isn't in either of their vocabularies. I thought Curtis didn't want anyone speaking with the media unless necessary," Victory said.

"It's necessary. Guess you haven't heard yet. Angel Hogan's uncle is a sergeant with CPD's Violent Crimes Squad."

"Shit." They'd be under even more pressure to solve The Wrapper case. She continued to watch the growing crowd of reporters and spectators. "Is Sean here?"

"Yeah." Ryan blew on his hands to help warm them, then stuffed them in his coat pockets. "Just waiting for some lights to be set up. It's pretty dark back there."

Victory yanked the collar of her coat up around her face to help with the frigid air nipping at her skin. "Who found her?"

"A jogger. He'd stopped for a breather before returning to his car," Ryan said.

"Who runs in this weather? It's close to freezing."

"Apparently, an exercise-obsessed freak."

She spotted Sean heading their way, drinking a Starbucks coffee. By the thick stubble on his face and the dark shadows under his eyes, he looked exhausted. She knew working homicide was a long grind and helping the FBI with The Wrapper and Eddie Bullington's case wasn't helping matters.

Sean handed her and Ryan a pair of Nitrile gloves. "They're ready for us."

She snapped on the gloves, her gaze straying from Sean and back to the throng of reporters. She still hadn't seen Melissa. Victory had never been at a crime scene in the past six years without the woman pestering her. "Let's stay clear of the media circus."

Sean nodded in agreement and pulled a flashlight from his jacket pocket.

After sneaking past the media, thanks to Curtis and Joe Mains busy getting in their five minutes of fame, Sean led the way. They trudged through the hilly terrain, the snow almost waist-high in spots. The flashlight's beam swung like a giant pendulum, sweeping the heavily wooded area.

Victory spotted the bright beams of light coming from the portable lights. She recognized members of the emergency response team standing next to the long cream-colored brick shelter. A group of uniformed officers were talking to Gregory and pointing while another group was busy combing the area for any evidence.

As she approached, Victory noticed a large shallow pond, not yet frozen over. Her breath clouded in the chilly air. "He could have dumped her anywhere. Behind the baseball diamond, the playground, back in the trees —"

"Or the hiking trails." Sean shut off the flashlight. "Any idea why a shelter is important to him?"

Frustration knotted her stomach. Victory shrugged, not knowing the answer. In the distance, she heard the loud hum of the generator powering the portable lighting. She veered off a short distance from the others and observed one of their response team techs photographing numerous boot prints in the snow while another tech was using snow wax, a specific casting compound used in the snow to make a form of the boot's tread. The footprints followed a path toward the shelter then disappeared in the snow.

A gust of wind whipped through the pine trees. Frantic wings rustled and flapped in the shadowy treetops canopying the area. When she returned to Sean and Ryan, she was horrified at what she saw. Nothing could have prepared her.

The putrid sweet smell of baby oil and burnt and rotting flesh invaded her senses first and lingered in the air. The victim's upper body was burnt so badly there wasn't much left except for chunks of bubble wrap, muscle, ligaments, and blackened skin hanging from her arms and upper torso. No hair was left on her head, the skin on her face, gone. All that was left, sunken and glazed-over-dead green eyes.

"Jesus." Ryan blinked a couple of times and looked away.

Sean held his ground. Victory could tell he was fighting to keep it together.

A charred breastplate and ribs revealed an open chest cavity. It appeared the killer had ripped out the heart. Victory grimaced. Bile rose in her throat. She staggered four or five steps away from the body and vomited in a snowbank next to a tree.

All eyes were on her. She could feel them. Twenty years on the job and she'd never been sick at a crime scene. A rookie move. She'd never live it down.

Gregory put his hand gently on her shoulder. "This one caught you off guard. It happens, Victory."

She straightened, sucked in long deep breaths, and then exhaled each one slowly and evenly. "He ripped out her heart," she said, her voice slightly wavering.

The M.E.'s eyes met hers. "It looks that way."

Ryan handed her a bottle of water. She took a couple of sips and searched Gregory's eyes. "We have to stop him."

"I found something during my examination that

might help." He gave her a small smile. "When you're ready."

She took another drink of water and waited for her stomach to stop whirlpooling.

"Has she been here long?" Sean asked, his eyes fixed on the grisly scene.

"Not long. Less than twenty-four hours. From the internal organs, I can see, they haven't started to decompose. I'll know a lot more once I do the post-mortem."

Victory braced herself, determined to continue, anxious to learn what the M.E. had discovered. "Show me what you found."

At the body, Gregory lowered to his knees in the snow and lifted the victim's right foot as best he could. He pointed a gloved finger at the bottom of the heel. "That's a product label from a box of Rohypnol embedded in a piece of melted bubble wrap."

The same drug the killer used to sedate his victims. Victory bent down and squinted at the discolored label with slightly smeared black lettering. At least most of what was left of the label was readable. "A partial serial number."

"The NDC number is missing, but we might have enough to trace it back to the original manufacturer."

She pushed her excitement down and glanced up at Ryan and Sean, cautiously optimistic, hoping it was more than wishful thinking that the killer had finally made a mistake. "We might have our first solid lead."

CHAPTER TEN

While they waited for the product label to be traced, Victory and Ryan walked up the steps leading to a two-storey house on Kinney Street with sand-colored vinyl siding and white trim, ten minutes from the University of Cincinnati where Angel Hogan had been enrolled. Snow fell like frozen confetti and blanketed the middle-class Evanston neighborhood.

Victory shivered, her pant legs still damp against her skin from hiking through the park. "Damn snow."

"They're calling for six to eight inches tonight and more tomorrow."

"Someone said snow arouses wonderful flashbacks of your childhood. Whoever said that was a dickhead." Her childhood was not a place Victory ever wanted to revisit.

Her father was a tough Cleveland detective, who'd worked out of the third district. He was also married to the bottle and enjoyed taking his stress out on her and her mother with his fists. It was back in the day when domestic and child abuse by police officers was virtually invisible. Victory had made the decision to leave home when she was seventeen and never looked back. Her mother, on the other hand, stuck it out, a decision Victory never understood. Two years after Jade was born, Victory received the phone call, a call she had predicted for years. Her father had shot and killed her mother, and then himself.

Ryan ran his fingers through his wet hair. "Guess you aren't into having a snowball fight."

She knew her partner was just trying to lighten things up after witnessing such a horrific image at the park. But Victory wasn't in the mood for his playful sense of humor. Not right now. Speaking with Angel Hogan's father wasn't going to be easy since they didn't have an ID on the body yet. They needed one. She'd have to prepare Angel's father for the worst, that his child was probably dead.

They stopped on the front porch. Multi-colored Christmas lights sparkled through the sheer curtains from the front window. A battery-operated holiday wreath made of garland, pinecones, and white LED lights glowed against the oak front door. Victory took a deep breath and knocked.

On the other side of the door, a dog barked wildly with excitement. Then the noise stopped, and the door opened. A man in his mid-forties with a kind face and vivid green eyes was holding an adorable brown puppy.

"Samuel Hogan. I'm Agent Victory McClane. This is my partner, Agent Slater."

The man's eyes snapped to her ID around her neck. "Did you find my daughter?"

His voice was frantic and filled with fear. She could tell he knew this wasn't a happy visit.

"May we come in?" Ryan asked.

He let them in and Victory noticed the man's hands were shaking when he closed the door. She glanced at a young girl sitting on the couch in the living room, watching a holiday TV show. She appeared to be about ten years old, and a spitting image of Angel. Dread flowed through Victory.

Samuel handed the dog to his daughter then picked up the remote and shut off the TV. "Sara, go watch the show in your bedroom, okay, sweetie? I need to speak with these people."

Worry flickered in the girl's eyes. She took the small dog and left the living room.

Samuel's gaze shifted from the stairs to Victory. "Have you found Angel?"

Victory paused for a few seconds and chose her words wisely. "A body was found in Rapid Run Park this evening. We don't know yet if it's your daughter or not."

He sat on the couch and dropped his face in his hands. "It could be someone else."

"There is a chance of that. We need to know for sure."

Samuel suddenly jumped to his feet. "I can come with you right now and see if it's Angel. It'll only take me a minute to get my neighbor to come over and watch Sara."

"I'm sorry, we can't do that, Mr. Hogan." Victory was about to strip a few more layers of hope from the man, and she didn't feel good about it. Part of her job included being as honest as possible based on what they knew so far. It was not a situation any parent should ever have to experience.

"What we need from you is Angel's hairbrush and toothbrush for a DNA sample."

The room grew deadly quiet.

"They're—upstairs in the bathroom. The blue toothbrush—and the red-handled hairbrush."

Ryan turned to Victory and lowered his voice a fraction. "I'll grab a couple of evidence bags."

Victory nodded. While Ryan went to the vehicle to get the bags, Samuel began to weep.

"I know this is extremely difficult." She'd noticed the living room didn't have any female personal touches. "Is your wife home?"

He shook his head slowly. "The kids' mother left four years ago. She had a drug problem. It's better that she's not around. She lives in California and hasn't talked to the girls since she walked out the door."

"I'm sorry."

"Do you think it's Angel?"

Victory looked at him, his eyes searching hers for the answer. She saw the pain. She wanted to tell him, to give him some type of closure but she couldn't. Not until they had the DNA results, even though she was certain the body was the man's daughter. "Let's wait and see what the DNA has to say."

After Ryan returned with the evidence bags, he headed upstairs. When he was out of sight, Samuel sat back down on the couch, the reality of the situation obvious on the man's anguished face.

"What am I supposed to tell, Sara? She's young and doesn't understand. She already thinks her big sister left like her mother. I don't know what to tell her."

Victory swallowed the hard lump forming in her throat and regret swamped her. She thought about Josh and what she wished she had told him when she'd dropped him off at the bank. "Tell her you love her."

Heavy footsteps thumped on the stairs. Ryan appeared with the evidence bags containing Angel's personal items.

Victory's gaze switched from her partner and back to Mr. Hogan. The man was silent, staring at the wall, his eyes vacant and tear-filled.

She tried to remain stoic even though her heart was breaking for him. "We'll contact you as soon as we have the results." Before leaving, she placed her business card on the coffee table, unsure if the grieving father heard one word of what she had said.

Outside, snow continued to fall, a thick curtain of white, turning the city into a winter wonderland. Wind rushed at her and snow lashed at her face. They got into the Suburban and Ryan started the engine. Frigid air pumped out of the heating vents.

Victory gazed at the evidence bags on the seat. "After we get those back to the lab and get the results, I want to swing by Melissa Mann's house."

Ryan raised an eyebrow. "Seriously?"

"I know. I can't believe I just said that either."

"Still no word from the troll—um—reporter?"

Victory yanked the seatbelt over her shoulder and secured it. "Nothing. She wasn't at the crime scene either. Yet another mystery to add to our plate." She watched the snow hitting the windshield. The flakes were hypnotizing and making her tired.

"That is strange. She's an ambulance chaser, always in our way at every crime scene." Ryan checked the side mirror and waited for a slow-moving car to pass before he steered away from the curb. "Maybe she doesn't want to be found because she's pulling your leg about having info about Bullington."

❅   ❅   ❅

At the coroner's office, Victory and Ryan took the elevator to the third floor where most of the labs were located, including, DNA, drug, trace, and ballistics. She knew most crime labs in the country were backlogged including Quantico's state-of-the-art facility. Hamilton County Coroner's Laboratory was no exception, serving forty-three police agencies in the region, as well as the City of Cincinnati. The business of death was a twenty-four-seven job.

The elevator doors opened.

Ryan paused and sniffed the air. "Smells like one of the lab techs is drying marijuana in the closet again."

"Or smoking it." Victory unzipped her coat.

Dawn Addison, a DNA tech met them in the hallway lined with evidence boxes waiting to be checked in. She was a pretty woman in her early forties with pale skin framed by shoulder-length wavy red hair. She looked tired and worn, her expression strained. Everyone involved with The Wrapper and the Bullington cases had been working tirelessly for days.

Victory handed her the evidence bags, her thoughts drifting to Angel Hogan's father. "Thanks for doing this on short notice. I know how busy you are."

Dawn took the bags. "Perfect timing. Gregory sent up a sample from the victim a little while ago. I should have the results within an hour or so."

Wheels clicked, jingled, and squeaked on the outdated and scuffed linoleum floor behind her. Victory glanced over her shoulder and watched a man pushing a dolly into the elevator, stacked high with boxes. She turned her attention back to Dawn. "Thanks. We'll stick around. We could use a break, a little downtime."

"It sounds like it's been crazy the past few days with The Wrapper and the Bullington cases."

"Unfortunately, the craziness is just beginning."

Dawn frowned and held up the bags. "Well, I'd better get started if you want the DNA results tonight."

"We'll be around. Thanks again."

After the woman left, Victory's stomach rumbled loudly.

Ryan grinned. "Now that's what happens after you spill your guts at a crime scene."

"I knew that was coming," Victory said. "It was just a matter of when. You aren't going to let me live that down, are you?"

Ryan smirked. "Not a chance."

She opened her mouth about to say something when her cell phone shrilled. She slipped it out of her pocket and answered the call.

"Hi, Sean."

"I just finished following up with the cab companies. No one matching Angel Hogan's description was picked up at the club."

"The killer probably met her inside."

"Looks that way," Sean said.

"Could you go back and talk to Angel's girlfriends again, and the club employees? I have a feeling someone knows something they aren't telling us. See if the club has cameras. And double-check every CCTV you can find in the area. We're at the lab waiting for Angel Hogan's DNA results, and a hit on the drug serial number."

"Sure. I'm downtown now, a couple blocks from the club," he said.

"Thanks."

After Victory finished the call, Ryan went across the street to a family diner and grabbed a couple of burgers and coffee. When he returned, she sat on the floor in the hallway, under the hum of the florescent lights and scarfed down her meal, satisfied the food would stop her grumbling stomach.

Ryan finished his burger, scrunched the wrapper into a ball, and tossed it in the bag.

"Vic, ever wonder how many bodies have come through this place?"

"Every time I'm sitting on the cold floor of a pot-smelling death house." She took a sip of her coffee and heard the elevator doors open at the end of the hallway, and saw Gregory walking toward them carrying a file folder. She rose to her feet.

The M.E. gave her a broad smile. "Good news."

"We could use some," Ryan said.

"The label was traced to a manufacturer in South Africa where the drug is legal."

"South Africa? The killer probably nabbed it on the streets since it's illegal here. How does that help us?"

"That doesn't." He handed her the file folder. "It's the partial print discovered on the corner of the label. We got a match. It belongs to a pharmacist by the name of Jeremy Elder. He owns a pharmacy downtown."

Ryan's eyes widened. "He screwed up. His fingerprints are on file, required by law."

Victory breathed a sigh of relief. It was the break they needed.

Gregory nodded. "The Ohio State Board of Pharmacy requires all pharmacists and interns submit a criminal records check including fingerprints."

She opened the folder and looked at the report. She examined the photograph of Jeremy Elder. He appeared to be in his thirties. He had striking male model looks, high cheekbones, and blue eyes. "He's attractive. If this is our man, he uses his looks to his advantage when hunting for his ideal victim."

Excitement filled her. She pushed it down, kept it at bay. She wouldn't be happy until the killer was proven guilty and put behind bars. At least they had enough for a warrant. She glanced at Ryan. "CenterTown Pharmacy on Race Street."

"I'll get Angie moving on the search warrant," Ryan said. He grabbed his cell phone and called the office.

"I'm going to check in with Dawn and see how out much longer for the DNA results." She looked at Gregory. "Thank you."

"My pleasure. If he is the killer, nail his ass to the wall, Victory."

She smiled slightly. "Believe me, that will be *my* pleasure."

With a spring in her step, Victory hustled down the hall. A muffled gunshot reverberated through the walls coming from the ballistics lab. Two doors down, she poked her head inside the cave-like confines of the DNA lab. Dawn was sitting at her makeshift desk, constructed from file cabinets and a slab of wood, working away on her laptop.

The woman looked up at her, her green eyes warier than earlier. "I was just about to come and see you. The DNA is a match." She closed the laptop and paused for a second. "Another young woman isn't going home."

A sick feeling rolled in Victory's stomach. Her excitement about Jeremy Elder sobered slightly, dampened by having to tell Samuel Hogan his daughter was dead.

* * *

Victory frowned at the traffic moving at a snail's pace due to the blizzard conditions. It had taken almost thirty minutes to reach downtown and they still weren't at the pharmacy. Ahead, a snowplow burst through the heavy snow on the street. The plow scraped against the pavement and tossed snow against the windshield of the Suburban.

Before they'd left the coroner's office, she had called Curtis to have another FBI agent go and notify Samuel Hogan about his daughter. She gazed out the window and watched the traffic creeping along in the other lane, her heart heavy.

Ryan turned the wipers on high. "What if he isn't our guy?"

"What?"

"What if he isn't our guy?"

"If he isn't, he's peddling Rohypnol out of the pharmacy. One way or another we're bringing him in."

"There was no home address listed in the file the M.E. gave us."

"I know, Riddle Man. I'm way ahead of you. Our response team is already on their way to his home on Flyer Drive."

Ryan huffed out a laugh, clearly amused by being called Riddle Man. "That's about thirty minutes from the field office. He drummed his fingers against the steering wheel. "What about Melissa?"

"She's a riddle that's going to have to wait to be solved." Victory pointed ahead to CenterTown Pharmacy's large red sign, blinking *'Open 24 Hours'*. Anticipation flowed through her, and her pulse rate accelerated. "That's the place."

The pharmacy was tucked between a mom-and-pop pizza joint and a small bakery. Both were closed. She'd called Sean when they had left the coroner's office, asking him to meet them with four Cincinnati cops in case there was trouble.

Ryan rolled into the unplowed lot and parked next to one of the three cars covered with snow. He kept the engine running. "Doesn't look too busy."

"That's good for us." Victory undid her seatbelt and her phone buzzed. She pulled the phone out of her pocket and read the text message. "Boot treads belong to a pair of Sorel Glacier boots, double E, size 12." She quickly forwarded the information to the FBI team en route to Jeremy Elder's house, then stuffed the phone into her pocket.

Ryan glanced at her. "Hey, you're forty-five tomorrow."

"Did you have to remind me? Forty-five. I demand a recount. The only good thing happening tomorrow is Jade coming home."

"And we might catch The Wrapper." Ryan released his seatbelt and smirked. "Did you know forty-five is three-hundred and fifteen years in dog years?"

Victory groaned inwardly and glanced at the clock on the dash, which read ten o'clock. Snow and ice pellets tapped gently against the windshield and melted almost instantly.

"What's the big plan for tomorrow evening?"

"Dinner and drinks at my place since everyone is hellbent on celebrating my forward movement into a nursing home."

The corners of his eyes crinkled in amusement and he gave her a toothy grin. "Someone has to celebrate, Vic." He turned the heat down and opened the window a bit. "I haven't seen Jade in a while."

"I hate to admit—she'll be happy to see you."

Victory thought about how proud she was of her daughter working hard in her first year in the criminal justice program at Notre Dame College. As much as she didn't want Jade following in her footsteps, Victory accepted her daughter wanted a career with the FBI. There was no stopping her. She stared out the window and the same nagging sadness filled her, knowing Josh wouldn't be seeing Jade graduate...get married...have kids.

"They're here," Ryan said.

"What?"

Her attention shifted to the side mirror as Sean's black SUV came rolling into the parking lot with two Cincinnati police cruisers following behind.

Ryan killed the engine.

After Sean and the officers exited their vehicles, Victory and Ryan went to meet them.

She nodded at the four male officers, their CPD knit caps covered in white, slick with snow. "Thanks for your help."

"Anytime. You think this guy is The Wrapper?" The tallest officer in the group asked as he unzipped his winter coat, revealing his black body armor.

Ryan nodded, glancing at the pharmacy. "We hope so."

"Would be nice to have the piece of crap off the streets," one of the other officers said.

Victory couldn't agree more. She turned her body to

shield herself from the driving wind and snow. "We have a team heading to his house. We'll know soon if he's the killer."

As they walked through the front door of the pharmacy, the air thrummed with tension and a blast of warm air hit her face. Victory looked around. The pharmacy was familiar. She swore she'd been here before but couldn't remember when. She let the thought go, focusing on hoping they had the right guy, then at least one serial killer would be off the streets.

The store was quiet. A lone female clerk was working the front checkout, ringing a young female customer's purchase through.

Victory, Ryan, and two of the officers cautiously walked to the back of the pharmacy while two officers stood guard at the front of the store.

Victory stopped in front of the glass-enclosed pharmacy counter with a small metal speaker. "Is Jeremy Elder here?"

The short woman in her thirties, dressed in a white lab coat, eyed Victory's FBI credentials hanging around her neck. The small plastic nametag pinned to the woman's coat read, *Malynda Beran*, with *Pharmacy Assistant* below her name.

Malynda's eyes widened. "Um—no, he's not. Is there something I can help you with?"

Ryan peered down the two aisles. "You sure he isn't here?"

The woman looked at Ryan, then back to Victory. "He left a few hours ago." She paused for a second and worry lines crinkled her forehead. "Is something wrong?"

"It's not something we can discuss."

"What's back there?" Ryan asked as he pointed to a closed gray door next to the pharmacy area.

"That's the storage room and our break room."

Victory nodded to the two officers to check out the rooms.

The woman straightened and pursed her lips. "Are you sure you're allowed to go back there without Jeremy here?"

Victory locked eyes with the woman. "I'm sure."

Sean handed Malynda the warrant he'd picked up on the way to the pharmacy.

She unfolded the paper and read it. Her eyebrows raised, and she put the warrant on the counter. "Could you please tell me what's going on? I've worked for Jeremy for almost six years."

"Sorry, we can't do that," Ryan said.

Victory's eyes traveled to the security camera in the corner of the ceiling. "Are there any other employees working tonight, besides you and the clerk at the front?"

Malynda shook her head. "No, it's extremely quiet with the storm."

"What time did Jeremy leave tonight?"

"About seven o'clock."

When the officers returned from checking the storage room, one of them shook his head.

"Was Jeremy here all day?"

"I don't know. I came in for my shift at three. As far as I know, he started work at six this morning like he always does." Victory was about to ask another question when her phone rang. She snatched the phone out of her pocket. It was one of their team members at Jeremy's house.

"Is he there?" Victory asked.

"Sorry, Vic. No sign of him. According to his neighbors, they haven't seen him today."

Victory recognized Mike Andrews' low, raspy voice. He was one of the agents she'd trained with when she first joined the Bureau. He had a foul mouth, a seventies handlebar mustache, and a tough beat cop attitude.

"We found some jewelry hidden in an envelope under the dresser in the bedroom. We've got a white gold ring that looks like the one belonging to Nicole Henderson. I'll email you the photo in a minute," he said.

Her excitement resurfaced. Jeremy Elder was looking more and more like he was The Wrapper. "Thanks. Did the Sorel boots turn up?"

"No boots. He's probably wearing them."

"Probably, or he tossed them." All they had to do was find him. Her gaze flicked back to the security camera. "Do me a favor, Mike. Get the ERT over to Center-Town Pharmacy on Race Street when they're done at the house."

"They're just finishing up," Mike said. "Might be a while before they get there with this shitty weather."

"It's going to be a long night, either way, bad weather or not. Also, have a couple of our guys sit on the house in case Elder returns."

"Will do."

Victory disconnected and turned to Ryan. She kept her voice to a whisper so Malynda couldn't hear her. "We'll need an arrest warrant for Jeremy Elder."

❋　❋　❋

With gloved hands, Jeremy bent and picked up the bloody heart from the warehouse floor and tossed the organ into the plastic garbage bin. Then he scooped up the HazMat suit, booties, and gloves he'd worn when he killed Angel. Hatred kept him focused. He wished it had been Lily's heart. She would have felt the same agony he'd felt when she left him and disappeared.

He could still smell the faint odor of baby oil, smoky burnt flesh, and body fluids over the strong odor of bleach he'd poured on the concrete floor earlier. He threw the chair, the woman's clothing, and her purse into the trash. The necklace she'd been wearing, a small gold cross, was tucked in his pocket for safekeeping—a nice addition to the other trophies he'd collected over the years.

His cell phone rang. Jeremy pulled the phone from his jeans pocket and checked the screen. It was his pharmacy assistant. He tapped the 'answer' button, drew a deep breath, and blew it out. He needed to sound calm as if it were business as usual.

"Hello?"

"Jeremy?"

Malynda's voice sounded odd. Something in her tone. Urgency.

"Is everything okay at work?"

"The FBI is here. They had a search warrant. They're going through the pharmacy right now. What's going on, Jeremy?"

His heart stopped, and he heard himself gasp. The FBI was on to him. Agent McClane was on to him. How? He'd been so careful right down to the smallest detail to ensure there wasn't a speck of evidence linking him to any of the women. There was a taste in the back of his throat, a combination of fear and anger. He paced the empty space with his cell phone gripped tight in his hand.

"Where are you?"

"In the bathroom, so they can't hear me."

Jeremy stopped pacing. He stared at the garbage pail. Evidence needed to be destroyed, and quickly. What was he going to do? He couldn't go to the pharmacy, and by now the authorities knew where he lived.

"I'll be in for my usual shift and I'll speak with them then. I have no idea what's going on," he said, knowing going into work was the last thing he was going to do. "Don't tell them we spoke, okay?"

"I've known you for years, Jeremy. You're a good man. I'm sure this is a misunderstanding."

"I'm sure you're right. Maybe some of the narcotics were mislabeled or something. It's happened before from the manufacturer. I'll look after it when I get there. Thanks for calling, Malynda. I appreciate it."

After Jeremy ended the call, he snatched the floor mop and threw it like a javelin across the warehouse. The handle hit the wall with a sharp crack. He felt his breathing speed up and the vein in the side of his neck thumped.

Getting caught wasn't an option. He'd never have the chance to find Lily and punish her. Anger raged through him. He kicked the metal bucket full of water and bleach, the contents splashing onto his pants as the bucket clattered against the cement floor.

He couldn't leave the country with the FBI on this trail. He had been prepared for years in case something like this happened. He had everything he needed at the warehouse. His eyes shifted to the Toyota Camry, registered in his dead mother's name. The FBI would be looking for his silver Acura.

The noose was tightening around him, squeezing,

suffocating him, and it didn't feel good. It wasn't over yet, though. Jeremy knew what needed to be done.

* * *

Derrick clipped the identification card to his shirt pocket as The Secret Service vehicle passed through Gate 3, on the west side of the army base near Annapolis and Reece Roads, an area reserved for Department of Defense identification holders.

Derrick looked at his father. "I haven't been back here in about seven years."

They drove past the sprawling glass and steel building that housed the National Security Agency, as well as the U.S. Cyber Command, a centralized command center for cyberspace operations. It was used to defend the information security environment, beefing up the DoD's cyber expertise to withstand, and respond to, a cyber-attack.

His father nodded, staring forward. "A lot has changed since then."

"I can see that."

"Mainly the explosion of high-end residential properties outside of Fort Meade. Urbanization at its finest. And of course, the centralization of services—the DAAF."

Derrick remembered reading a few years back that The Defense Adjudication Activities Facility was now home to all the adjudicative offices of the DoD, including personnel security investigations regarding eligibility to occupy and access national security and classified information.

"Budget cuts, son. Slice and consolidate is the name of the game between the power players."

"Are Evelyn Cobb and Colonel Collier still running the Elara Project?"

A low-flying plane's engines rumbled and whined, preparing to land at Tipton Airport, south of Fort Meade.

His father nodded. "Both have always been huge supporters of the project, as you know. The president wouldn't have it any other way. He trusts them to keep the project always moving forward and under the radar."

As they drove through the sprawling base, Derrick spotted the movie theater where he'd hung out at least twice a week while perfecting his paranormal skills. He remembered the first movie he'd watched: *"Reservoir Dogs"*.

After their driver parked behind the Department of Defense Consolidated Adjudications Facility, the DoD CAF as it was known, Derrick and his father got out of the vehicle and walked to the back door of the three-floor white building with red brick and towering white pillars. The structure looked exactly as Derrick remembered it. A harsh north wind blew and spit snow in his face.

Derrick turned his face out of the wind. "Any idea what type of special skill this new recruit has? The president sounded excited."

His father grinned. "This one you'll have to see to believe."

❋   ❋   ❋

Inside the 151,000-square-foot facility, two hulking male soldiers carrying M16A4s and dressed in two-tone brown fatigues stood like statues on either side of the private elevator that lead to the basement where the Elara Project was located. After one of the soldiers checked their IDs, Derrick and Roland entered the elevator. Roland pressed the button for B1. The doors quietly slid closed.

To outsiders and employees of the ten agencies lodged within the facility, the basement contained another arm of the DoD's consolidated services. No one was the wiser.

Moments later, the elevator dinged, and the doors spread open. They stepped into the wide, brightly lit corridor. Directly across from them was a metal door marked 'Authorized Personnel Only' in big bold red lettering. Roland placed his right thumb on the screen of the keypad lock. The lock buzzed as it scanned his fingerprint, then beeped three times before the screen flashed green. He turned the knob and opened the door. They walked around the corner and stopped in front of another door with a retinal scanner.

"I see you've upgraded security," Derrick said.

His father leveled his eyes at the scanner and waited. "Can't be too careful, considering what's going on behind door number two." The lock clicked loudly, then the thick metal door automatically swung open.

Dr. Evelyn Cobb, the project's scientist for over twenty years, greeted them in the cozy reception-like area that looked like a living room, complete with a couch and a seventy-inch TV mounted on the wall. Derrick remembered spending a lot of his free time in the room with the other recruits.

Her blue eyes twinkled as she smiled. "Derrick. It's wonderful to see you."

"You too, Evelyn. It's been a few years."

The woman hadn't aged a day since he'd seen her

last. In her mid-fifties, she looked as if she were in her thirties, the way her short brown hair was cut in a pixie style, framing her smooth porcelain skin. She was wearing casual street clothes under a white lab coat.

She shot a sideways glance at Roland. "You need to bring this guy around more often."

"I'll certainly try."

Derrick shrugged off his coat and set it on the L-shaped leather couch. "Where's the colonel?"

"Richard is out of town headhunting until next week. He'll be sorry he missed you." She blew out a breath. "Well, come on. I have lots to show you."

Derrick and his father followed Evelyn into the main area of the project. The space was spotless. It looked like a giant lab with brushed steel, whitewashed walls, and pristine white flooring. The bank of tall arched windows that once flooded with sunlight had been covered with a dozen glass soundproof chambers. On the other wall housed workstations, computers, monitors, cameras, and scientific equipment.

Evelyn stopped at the first chamber.

Derrick peered through the glass at an attractive blonde-haired woman sitting next to a man with brown hair cropped short around his ears. Both were wearing black headphones and had their eyes closed. Every few minutes their eyes would open, then they would feverishly write down information and close their eyes again.

"We're still using remote viewers?" Roland asked.

"For specific assignments. Mia and Adam are our most accomplished recruits, experts in the field of RV. They've been able to locate classified documents in Russia, Iran, and North Korea, that contained nuclear program details, as well as data confirming possible terrorist attacks and plots to assassinate President Burke. Everything we do is still monitored closely by Richard and verified on the ground, the same way it was done when Derrick was with us."

Derrick moved to the next glass enclosure. Evelyn and his father stood behind him.

"This is Elisha Murphy. She's one of ours, a sergeant with the military. She's been with the Elara project for two months now. Elisha is an omni-linguist. She can understand any form of language. She'll be used on the ground in various countries."

"A pretty handy skill to have," Roland said.

They continued to move down the line.

"Neil Frader manipulates dreams. I'm sure you've both heard about a certain female dignitary in Pakistan who recently died of a sudden and unexplained heart attack."

"That was Neil's doing?" Derrick asked.

Evelyn nodded.

In the next glass chamber, a thin man was sitting at a table across from another man who appeared to be twice his age.

"Troy Cruz is the younger one with dark hair. His expertise is ESP. He uses it to interrogate enemies without the use of drugs or torture. He's already been in the field for the CIA at various black sites around the world."

"This group appears older than many of the original recruits twenty years ago," Derrick said.

"They are. The median age is twenty-eight. Some of the paranormal skills we've used have changed since the Cold War Era, depending on our needs. Some of our recruits are required to be older, like in Troy's case. We can't send a sixteen-year-old to a black site and be taken seriously. In your case, Derrick, you don't need to be in public to be able to use your abilities, so age never mattered."

Roland glanced at Evelyn. "Remind me not to piss off any of these recruits."

"I think you're safe." She winked. "The Elara Project continues to be the crème de la crème, a free-for-all of super paranormal powers geared to protect the security of the United States. Quality over quantity. The way it should be. The way it has been in the past. We have a nineteen-year-old joining us next week who uses psionic blast."

Derrick raised an eyebrow. "I didn't think that was possible."

Psionic blast wasn't something he'd thought was real. If it was, overloading a person's mind could cause extreme pain, memory loss, unconsciousness, and even death. It was a skill not unlike his own, as the talent could be operated remotely, but that's where the similarity ended.

"Scientifically, there isn't any explanation as to how psionic blast works, as far as brain function is concerned. No one thought what you, your father, or grandfather could do was possible either. You've proved all the scientific nay-sayers wrong."

Derrick nodded. "Good point."

Evelyn led them past the remaining empty glass chambers and opened a metal door at the end of the space. Inside the smaller space, a bald-headed muscular man in his twenties, wearing heavy black-framed glasses, was sitting on a couch playing an Xbox game.

"There he is. Meet Nathan Jacenko, our newest recruit. He's only been here for a week."

Nathan set the game controller beside him and stood. "Hi."

"This is Derrick, and his father, Roland."

Nathan gave them a small smile.

"They're here to learn more about your special ability."

"It's different from the others," he said. "Really different."

Derrick noticed a sadness in Nathan's voice as he spoke. He could tell the kid thought of himself as a freak, just like Derrick had felt long before he'd first joined the Elara Project. But it hadn't taken Derrick long to relax, and realize he wasn't the only one who had felt that way.

"Have you rested enough to give them a short demonstration?" Evelyn asked.

Nathan nodded again. "Sure."

He entered the separate metal chamber, built differently from the rest, with a rectangular glass viewing window. Derrick stepped up to the window and waited. A mannequin and various other items were in the room; a half dozen big red balls and firewood were stacked in the center of the room.

"Seems like a nice kid," Roland said to Evelyn.

"He's quieter than the others, sticks to himself more than I'd like. It's an adjustment being here away from family and friends."

"Being different isn't easy. He'll come around. It'll take time," Derrick said, knowing better than anyone.

Evelyn nodded to Nathan. He turned and stared at the stack of firewood. Seconds later, each piece of wood caught fire. Then a candle on a small table lit.

Derrick's eyes widened. He'd witnessed a lot of things that defied scientific explanation. "Pyrokinesis."

"I told you, son, you'd have to see it to believe it."

Evelyn's eyes sparkled with pride and excitement as she watched the young man.

Derrick stared and concentrated his energy at one of the balls. It lifted slowly off the floor and into the air. Nathan targeted his energy at the ball. It burst into flames.

"There is no scientific evidence suggesting this phenomenon is real, that the brain can trigger explosions of fire. As you can see, it is very real."

"This is why the Elara Project is so important and why if anyone threatens it, they need to be stopped immediately," Roland said.

Derrick knew his father's comment was directed at him, regarding Eddie Bullington and Melissa Mann.

No one spoke as they continued to observe, mesmerized as Derrick moved the objects inside the room with his mind while Nathan set each of the items on fire, disintegrating them.

Derrick felt his father's hand heavy on his shoulder.

"Looks like you might have some serious competition, son."

CHAPTER ELEVEN

Six hours later, Victory and Ryan left the pharmacy. The snow had stopped, and the roads were clear. Victory rested her head against the headrest and closed her eyes. Exhaustion had set in. They had been going non-stop for days and another all-nighter was taking a toll. The hum of the Suburban's engine was making her sleepier.

Hundreds of cops and FBI agents in Cincinnati and Cleveland were searching for Jeremy Elder. He wouldn't be able to hide for long with his face plastered on TV and all over on the internet. The ERT had discovered a dozen boxes of Rohypnol stashed at the pharmacy. It was beginning to make sense. He used his looks to pick up his victims then used the odorless and tasteless date rape drug to kidnap and keep his victims sedated until he killed them. For the first time in almost a decade, Victory felt some satisfaction, knowing they finally knew who The Wrapper was. A pharmacist, of all people. She couldn't wait to question the man. She was betting Jeremy Elder loved to talk about himself a lot. Serial murderers often did.

"You want a coffee? Ryan asked.

She half-opened her eyes and yawned. Her head felt thick and foggy from a lack of sleep. "Yes. Caffeine solves everything. We still have to make a quick stop at Melissa's house to solve the next riddle before I crash for a few hours and Jade comes home and the annual festivities begin."

"Happy Birthday, Vic. It's official. You're old."

"Great. Thanks. Your time is coming."

"Come on. It's not that bad. Feel any older?"

"Just call me Grandma McClane." Victory yawned again. "Where's my rocking chair?"

Ryan laughed. He slowed the Suburban and stopped at the red light. "What are you going to do about Derrick and the flower situation?"

"According to you, I'm now old which makes me wiser than you. I'll take care of it. You'll be the first to know...well the second." Her eyes closed.

Ryan floored the vehicle.

The forward jolt from him accelerating away from the traffic light forced her eyes open. Victory glared at him for a good fifteen seconds. "You did that on purpose."

"Gotta keep you and your old bones awake." He steered into the coffee shop drive-through.

At a quarter to seven, the small coffee shop wasn't busy. There was only one car ahead of them.

"Since it's a special day, I'll even buy your coffee," Ryan said.

"Nice guy. In that case, I'll take a chocolate glazed donut too."

"You want a candle on it?"

She shook her head. "Obviously, you're as tired as I am."

After going through the drive-through, Ryan drove

out of the parking lot.

"Where are we heading?"

"Monticello Avenue." She took a drink of her coffee, savoring it, needing the hit of caffeine in a big way.

Ryan turned onto I-75 and drove north.

"Why do you think Elder killed all those women?"

Victory fell silent and weighed her partner's question for a long moment. Someone had made Jeremy Elder angry, furious enough to take it out on eight innocent women in a most sickening and demented way. The baby oil and bubble wrap reminded the killer of someone and something about a park compels him to kill. "Somewhere along the line, someone close to him pissed him off. A woman. He's making a very conscious decision to kill. She's the real target of his rage. Pure payback."

"Hope we find him soon."

Through exhaustion and fog, the long days had blended together, and she wasn't sure what day it was. Then it dawned on her. "The tenth anniversary of his first kill is tomorrow, Ryan." Victory didn't like that the killer was still out there, and they didn't know where he was. She ate her donut and stared out the front window. They weren't any farther along in the case then they were twenty-four hours ago, other than they knew the killer's name.

"If we don't nab him, expect another body to turn up sometime tomorrow. He's a creature of habit. The anniversary is important to him, means everything to him. He has to kill even if it means he'll get caught or killed," Victory said.

"Just when I thought we were ahead of the game."

"It ain't over till it's over."

"Yogi Berra."

"You're one smart cookie this early."

Thirty minutes later, the sun crept above the horizon and Ryan maneuvered the Suburban onto Monticello Avenue.

Victory straightened in the seat and gazed out the window. "It's the gray brick ranch halfway up the block on the left." All she wanted to do was get this part of the day done, go home, take a hot shower, and sleep. By the time they reached Melissa's house, the caffeine and sugar fix had kicked in giving her a shot of energy.

Victory watched as a dark blue Jaguar F-Pace SUV parked in front of the house. The male driver got out and looked up and down the street as if he was looking for something or someone. Then he walked toward the front door.

Victory squinted in the glaring sunlight through the windshield. "Wait. Is that?" She squinted again. "Derrick Lynn?"

"What is he doing here?" Ryan asked, as he wheeled the vehicle in the driveway and parked.

She climbed out of the SUV and shut the door, harder than she normally would.

Derrick turned. His eyes widened, and his mouth fell open. He appeared bewildered.

"What are you doing here, Mr. Lynn?" Victory asked.

"Call me, Derrick." He smiled and put his hands in his coat pockets. "I have an interview with Melissa Mann."

"At her house? This early?" Ryan asked, obviously not convinced.

"She called my office yesterday and said to come by the house this morning to go over everything before she did a feature on Dragon's Drought next week. She wanted to get the prep work done before going to the station."

There was a beat of silence between the three of them before Derrick spoke again, his gaze locking with Victory's. "It's nice to see you again."

She hated to admit it, but she was strangely happy to see him. Victory said nothing and continued her silent observation. Her gaze veered to the unshoveled walkway leading to the front door. It looked as if Melissa hadn't been in or out of the house for days. Store sale flyers and other mail partially hung out of the mailbox and flapped in the chilly air.

She glanced at her partner. "Check the garage and see if her car is here. It doesn't look like she's left the house for days."

While Ryan investigated the garage, Victory tried to get a better read on Derrick, unsure if what he told them was true. She had done a background check on him after their first meeting and nothing earth-shattering had turned up. Her stomach felt tight, the same feeling she had when she first met the man as if he was hiding something. She had questions, lots of them, like how he had gotten her home address. Behind her, Ryan's voice carved through her thoughts.

"Her car's here, Vic."

Something felt wrong, off. Melissa was a woman who would stop at nothing to get a story. Victory doubted the reporter had decided to sit at home for days and especially stop answering phone calls.

"I'll check the back of the house," Ryan yelled, as he rounded the corner of the garage.

Victory walked past Derrick to the front door. He was wearing an expensive leather coat and she caught a whiff of his aftershave. The clean and woodsy scent suddenly reminded her of her husband. She pushed the memory away and glanced at Derrick.

"Stick around until we speak with Melissa."

"Sure. Whatever you want."

After knocking several times and no one answered, Victory turned the doorknob on the off-chance it was unlocked. It wasn't. She plodded through the snow and peered through the front window. There was no movement inside.

Ryan came around the corner of the house, the bottom of his pants stained and wet from the snow. "Everything's locked uptight. No sign of her."

Victory heaved a heavy sigh. She grabbed her phone from her pocket and dialed the reporter's number. The call went to voicemail right away. "Something isn't right." She hung up and pulled out her gun.

Ryan drew his weapon.

Derrick's gaze wandered past her to the front door. "What's going on?"

"Stay put." She hoofed it to the front door. Ryan followed and held open the screen door.

Two-handing her gun, Victory lifted her right leg and kicked the door with the heel of her boot. Wood cracked, and the doorframe buckled. A dog barked in the distance. She kicked again, harder. The door flew open. Victory raised her gun and cautiously headed inside.

✳   ✳   ✳

Derrick leaned against his SUV and rubbed his hands together to warm them. He knew what Victory would find inside. Things weren't looking good for him.

He had to get the reporter's laptop before anyone discovered her notes about the Elara Project. If he didn't, the house of cards would crash down, taking him out, his father, and the president. It was bad enough the reporter and Bullington were connected and they were both dead.

It was supposed to be easy. Break-in. Grab the laptop. Go.

Bad timing. Running into two FBI agents was the last thing he thought would happen. He wanted to jump in his SUV and take off. He'd thought about it. He couldn't. He'd look guiltier than he already was.

Victory was becoming a huge threat. Derrick grabbed his phone from his pocket and dialed his father.

"What is it, son? I'm heading out the door to meet with the president."

"I'm at the reporter's house. No way I can get the laptop." He explained to his father what was going on as he watched two Cincinnati police cruisers speeding down the street toward him.

"FBI agents? Bad timing, indeed."

There was a long beat of silence.

"I'll look after it from my end, but you'll need to take care of any potential fallout."

Derrick wasn't sure what fallout his father was talking about, nor did he care as long as the laptop ended up in their possession.

"I'll call you back with the details."

Derrick shoved the phone into his pocket and walked slowly back to the front door of the house, his nerves on edge, concerned what was going to happen next. He had to remain calm and play dumb. He heard Victory's muffled voice coming from inside the house then more sirens closing in fast from the west.

* * *

Victory's good mood evaporated along with the sugar high. Her stomach did a flip-flop. She put a hand over her mouth and nose. "Open a window before I toss my birthday donut."

The master bedroom reeked of urine, feces, something that smelled like nail polish remover mixed with maple syrup and rotten meat.

Ryan flashed a grin. "Wouldn't be the first time."

She ignored the comment, his reminder that she had tossed her cookies at the crime scene was aging faster than she was.

He unlocked the window and opened it a few inches, enough to help stabilize the vile stench, but not enough to disturb any possible evidence. "That's just nasty. Guess your gut was right."

Victory stared down at Melissa's lifeless body on the bed and the red and purple ligature mark around her neck. Lengthy, deep scratches from her long nails marked her neck and face in a desperate plea to save herself. Her eyes were wide, the whites, blood red. Her body was partially buried within a thick white and gray satin duvet. Her bare feet were hanging out.

"I have some information about Eddie Bullington's death. It's important."

Important enough to kill for it.

A belt from a floral satin bathrobe, an alarm clock, and a shattered wineglass were splayed on the floor. An expensive designer lamp was toppled over on the nightstand.

"She put up a fierce struggle," Ryan said.

Victory nodded and thought for a moment. "Bring Derrick inside. Plant him somewhere, the living room, office. I want to talk to him."

"You think he had something to do with this? Might be just a wrong place at the wrong time scenario. We watched him arrive a couple minutes before we did."

All Victory knew was the man was here and Melissa was dead. She wasn't happy where her thoughts were heading. That connected him to both cases even if he hadn't killed Melissa or Nicole. At the very least his timing at the house was suspicious.

"He could've been in the house earlier, then came back."

"Maybe." Ryan thrust his hands into his pant pockets. "At least we know The Wrapper didn't do this one."

That should have been comforting but it wasn't. Melissa knew something about the Bullington case and it might have cost her life.

Ryan looked around the room. The place is locked up snug. "The Shadow?"

Victory shrugged. "We'll have to wait and see where the evidence takes us."

Sirens howled, and vehicle doors slammed shut outside the house. Voices floated inside the bedroom through the open window, the sound a confused muffled buzz.

After Ryan left to go get Derrick, Victory stood in the doorway and watched the bedroom flood with crime scene techs, taking notes, photographing, videotaping, and measuring. She made a quick call to Curtis to see if Jeremy Elder had been located yet. He hadn't. He was still out there, somewhere.

"Make sure her hands get bagged," Victory said to one of the crime techs walking into the bedroom.

He gave her a nod and got busy.

Victory walked down the hallway to the living room.

Derrick was seated comfortably on the couch, looking relaxed, watching the commotion. She heard Ryan talking to one of the local cops in the kitchen.

Derrick stood when she entered the room. "What's happening?"

"Melissa is dead." She waited for his reaction, hoping he'd give away something useful.

"Jesus. How?"

"That's not important. What is important, is how this looks."

His eyebrows came together in confusion. "What do you mean?"

"You're here. Melissa's dead. A causal association yet connected."

"I can assure you it is simply a coincidence."

"A heck of a coincidence," Ryan said from the doorway of the kitchen.

Derrick glanced at Ryan then back to Victory. He remained silent.

She searched his face. She wasn't getting any type of gut reaction from the man. Either he was telling the truth, or he was a world-class liar.

"How'd you get my home address to send the flowers?"

"This is really embarrassing." He let out a breath. "I had someone at the DoD get it for me."

Victory was taken back by the revelation and the length he had gone to to get her address, so he could send her flowers. "Your father?" Under the circumstances, she should have been creeped out. She wasn't, which baffled her.

"No."

"Whoever gave you my address, shouldn't have. I'm an FBI agent. If that information ever got—"

"I'm sorry. My lips are sealed. I just wanted to have dinner with you, that's why I sent the invitation with the flowers."

By the tone of his voice, he sounded genuinely sorry. Victory scrubbed an invisible speck of dirt from her coat then trained her gaze toward the front door. There were more questions she wanted to ask Derrick, but she was uncomfortable talking in front of her partner since she'd never told Ryan about the dinner invitation. Not that it was any of his business. Sometimes his brotherly love went too far. She knew he was only trying to protect her.

"You're free to leave. If we have any other questions, we'll be in contact."

On the way to the door, Derrick stopped beside her and smiled. "Maybe one day we'll have that meal together."

* * *

After sleeping for five hours, later that evening, Victory sat in the living room with Jade, drinking a glass of Cabernet Sauvignon. Ryan and Angie were in the kitchen, talking. The apartment smelled of tomato sauce, garlic, fresh basil, and cheese. The aroma made Victory's stomach growl. She hadn't had chicken parmesan since before Josh died. It was times like this that her husband's absence weighed heavily upon her. Tonight, she missed his culinary flair and his laughter.

"Happy Birthday, Mom," Jade said.

Victory smiled at her daughter. "Thanks, hun. I'm so

happy you're home for a couple of days."

"I'm glad exams are over with."

"I'm sure you did well. You always do. Your father would be proud. I know I am."

Jade looked up at the photographs of her father on the mantel. "Wish he was here."

The thought made Victory's heart squeeze. "Me, too."

"Do you think he's watching from heaven?"

Victory wasn't sure what to say after losing her faith in God when Josh was killed. In her mind, if there wasn't a God, heaven couldn't possibly exist. His death had ripped every shred of faith from her.

She took a drink of wine and glanced at her daughter, not wanting to disappoint her. "I'm sure he is."

"Where's Sean?" Ryan asked from the dining room.

Victory's eyes shifted to the colorful birthday banner taped to the wall with streamers and balloons next to the clock. "He should be here in a few minutes."

Jade glanced over her shoulder at Ryan then turned and whispered to Victory. "Those two are definitely doing it."

"What?"

"Ryan and Angie. They're doing it."

Victory laughed. "That obvious?"

Jade grinned and nodded.

The apartment buzzer went off. Jade bounced off the couch and went to let Sean in.

Victory got up and went to the kitchen to grab a beer. When she walked in, Ryan and Angie were in a sensual embrace. She cleared her throat, opened the fridge, and pulled out a bottle of beer.

She was happy Ryan had found someone he cared

about, Curtis wouldn't be thrilled. They'd have to figure out how they were going to make things work at the office.

"Sorry, Vic. Didn't know you were there," Ryan said.

Angie looked away, her cheeks pink with embarrassment.

Victory opened the bottle of beer and tossed the cap in the garbage. "You two think you can keep your hands to yourselves long enough to have dinner?" She stopped herself from smiling and walked out of the kitchen.

"Happy Birthday, Vic," Sean said, as he took off his coat and tossed it on the arm of the couch.

"Thanks, Sean." She handed him the bottle of beer.

"Can we eat now?" Jade asked.

"Sure," Victory said.

Sean slugged back a mouthful of beer. "Sorry, I'm late. I had a few things to do."

"You're here. That's all that matters." Victory smiled.

While everyone took a seat around the dining room table, Jade was in the kitchen loading everyone's plates with food.

Victory topped up her wine and set the empty wine bottle beside her. "Any news on Elder?"

Sean shook his head. "A few tips that didn't pan out. A BOLO was issued for his vehicle, a silver Acura TL."

Ryan took a drink of his beer. "Does he have any family?"

"An older brother. Patrick. He's an ER doc at Houston Methodist Hospital in Texas. Don't know if Jeremy has a girlfriend yet. Still working on that one. His mother died a few years ago."

Victory couldn't imagine the shock, learning your

brother was a serial killer. Nor could all the training or experience in the world prepare an agent to look into loved one's eyes and tell them their child was dead. Victory had done it so many times she'd lost count. She wished for once she could deliver some good news—like Jeremy Elder had been caught.

"Eight pieces of jewelry belonging to the victims were recovered," Sean said.

"Hey. No talking shop until after dinner," Jade said, as she handed Victory a plate of food.

No shop talk was one of Josh's rules when they were at the dinner table. Because of all their crazy schedules, it was important to savor the little family time they had together.

Victory eyed the chicken drenched in marinara sauce and cheese, and grilled carrots, tomatoes, and mushrooms. "Looks delicious."

Jade finished serving the others and sat down.

Ryan raised his beer in salute. "Happy Birthday, Vic. Cheers."

Everyone raised their drinks.

Victory grabbed her wine glass. "Just remember. I'm not forty-five. I'm eighteen with twenty-seven years of experience."

Everyone laughed.

"Dinner looks great. I don't remember the last time I had a real meal," Sean said, as he dug in.

"Jade made it, using her father's famous recipe. Victory took a bite of the chicken parmesan, the rich and tangy taste bringing back two decades of memories. She forced herself to keep it together.

After everyone finished dinner, Ryan handed her a thin gift-wrapped box with a big pink bow. "We got you a little something, Vic."

Angie and Ryan grinned at each other.

Victory slowly and suspiciously took the box then glanced at her daughter who was also grinning. "I'm afraid to open it."

"Come on, Mom. It won't bite you." Jade said. "Promise."

Victory's eyes narrowed at Sean. "You know anything about this?"

He shook his head. Victory knew better. They were all in on whatever was inside the box.

Victory unwrapped the box and opened it. Inside was a white bag. She held it up. On the front of the bag was printed in bold red lettering, 'Victory's Puke Bag'.

She burst out laughing, welcoming, and needing the distraction. "I knew I'd never live it down."

Sean laughed. "It'll go nicely with your work attire."

"Smartasses." Victory shook her head, staring at the bag. "Thank you. I think."

Jade stood and reached for her purse on the kitchen island. "Oh, I have something for you." She passed Victory a small black box. "I hope you like it."

"You didn't need to get me anything." Victory opened the box. It was a white-gold chain bracelet. "It's beautiful." She held the piece of jewelry up for everyone to see.

"It's so pretty," Angie said.

Jade lowered her head then looked up at Victory. Her eyes misted over. "It's special, Mom. I had it made from Dad's neck chain, the one he wore all the time."

Victory's heart skipped a beat. The room turned quiet as if everyone was holding their breath, waiting for her reaction.

She clutched the bracelet tighter. It was a piece of Josh she needed right now. Victory went and hugged her daughter. "Thank you."

Angie stood. "Time for cake." She went into the kitchen and brought the cake out with forty-five lit candles.

Victory put the bracelet on, then blew out the candles unaware of the vehicle parked across the street from her apartment building, watching and waiting.

CHAPTER TWELVE

On the east side of town, Derrick paced to stay warm as he waited inside the dark tunnel. Moonlight glinted through the pine trees cluttered tightly against each other, camouflaging the tunnel. At the other end of the tunnel, snow skipped across the street.

He was worried about his run-in with Victory at the reporter's house. Even though there was a lot of attraction between the two, Derrick, felt Victory was working behind the scenes, looking for dirt on him. She seemed too cool when she'd let him leave Melissa's house without questioning him any further. Then the phone conversation he had with his father earlier ran through his mind.

"What's the plan?" Derrick asked.

"Police corruption has run rampant throughout the city, and the state for that matter, for decades. Why not take advantage of the situation?"

"How?"

"A police officer will meet you at midnight in the old tunnel on the east side. Everyone has a price."

"What's his price? Can we trust him?"

"Five thousand. It won't matter if we can trust him or not."

His father gave him the officer's name and home address.

"You know what needs to be done after you've obtained the laptop. We obviously can't chance this coming back on us."

Derrick checked his watch then spotted a dark figure walking briskly toward him. The moon illuminated the figure as he drew closer. The man was about forty-years-old, short and heavy-set, wearing a black CPD toque and leather jacket. He had a laptop under his arm.

"This wasn't easy to get out of the evidence locker," the man said.

His voice was raspy, and he was struggling to breathe evenly. A life-long smoker, Derrick guessed.

He passed Derrick the laptop.

Derrick took it and handed him a white envelope filled with cash. "Thanks."

The officer fingered through the cash then stuffed the money in his jacket pocket.

"Are you sure this can't be traced back to me?"

Derrick shook his head. "You won't need to worry about that."

❈   ❈   ❈

Warm breath brushed against her cheek. His lips slid down the length of her neck. Then he looked at her...blue eyes...dark hair.

Victory jerked upright in the darkness of the bedroom, disoriented, her mind muddy from the wine she'd drank the night before. Goosebumps broke out over her bare arms and legs. Why was she dreaming about Derrick? The dream felt so real. It was as if he had been in her bedroom. She swung her legs over the edge of the bed and looked around the room, relieved she was alone. She glanced at the clock's red digits and let out a sigh. Six a.m. It was probably the wine, something she didn't drink often, combined with Josh not being around for her birthday. Or maybe Derrick's appearance at Melissa's house was still bothering her? It was as if he had been there for something other than an interview. His timing at Melissa's house stunk, felt wrong then, and still did.

After a quick shower, Victory got dressed, and put her gun in her holster then headed to the kitchen. She walked past the spare bedroom where her daughter was staying. The door was partially open. Jade probably wouldn't be awake until after Victory had gone to work. It was wonderful to have her home, even for a few days. And she'd be back the week before Christmas again, to celebrate the holidays for the second time without her father.

Victory hit the button on the coffee maker then padded to the hall and grabbed the newspaper delivered every morning outside her apartment door.

When she returned, she tossed the paper on the kitchen table and poured a cup of coffee. Her phone rang, and she cringed, hoping another body hadn't been discovered. She snatched the phone off the counter.

"You're up early, Vic," Ryan said.

"Too early."

"*Why* are you up? Usually, I'm the one dragging you out of bed."

Victory pulled out a chair and sat at the table, her eyes traveling to the front page of the newspaper, to the photograph of Jeremy Elder.

She lied. "I couldn't sleep. What's up?"

"Elder's Acura was found abandoned on Neeb Road."

"The guy isn't stupid." Another thought hit her. "That's about halfway between his house and where he dumped Angel Hogan's body."

"He might still be in the area."

"Have the locals and our guys quietly beef up their presence in the area." She heard Angie's voice in the background.

"I have to go, Vic. I'll pick you up around eight."

Victory set the phone down and skimmed the rest of the front page as she drank her coffee. Eddie Bullington's death had taken up less space this time around, only three sentences. Further down the page, another headline caught her attention.

CPD OFFICER FOUND DEAD FROM APPARENT SUICIDE...Randy Tiller, a ten-year veteran of the Cincinnati Police Department was found dead in his home early this morning...shot with his service pistol...

It was the fourth suicide to hit the CPD in the past six months. The officer's name was familiar. Victory was sure Sean had mentioned him during many of their conversations while working on The Wrapper case. Over one hundred law enforcement officers had taken their own lives the past year in the US and that number was modest. PTSD and depression were the top causes. More officers had died of suicide than from shootings and traffic accidents combined. The grim reality of a tough job working the streets.

She got up and set her mug on the counter, ready to pour another cup of coffee when a knock at the door startled her. Victory went to the door and peered through the peephole. Her pulse sped up when she saw who was on the other side. She ran her hands through her hair and checked herself in the small mirror, hanging next to the closet.

Another knock. This time louder.

As a precaution, her hand instinctively slid to her gun holster. Victory drew a deep breath and let it out. She unlocked the door and opened it partway, uncertain how she felt about letting him in. Part of her was angry he'd gotten into the apartment tower and past John. The other part was intrigued as to why Derrick Lynn was standing in her hallway.

She looked at him. His haunting blue eyes met hers and her breath caught in her throat for the second time in days. "How'd you get into the building?"

"Your doorman. He's a talkative guy. I think he's trying to play match-maker."

There was no telling what Derrick had told John to gain entry into the building, and Victory would be checking out Derrick's story. Her eyes shifted to the two large coffees in the tray in Derrick's hand, and the bag of freshly baked goods from one of her favorite bakeries, Chic Girl Sweets.

"Since you had to cancel our dinner plans, I thought I'd stop by with breakfast." He held up the paper bag. "Donuts, croissants, and muffins. The best I could come up with this early in the morning."

"You don't give up, do you?"

"No." He smiled. "Not with you."

After her dream about him, Victory stood there and debated for a long moment. She finally gave in and opened the door. "Come on in. I'll take those."

He passed her the tray of coffee and baked goods.

While Derrick took off his coat and boots, out of the corner of her eye, she caught her wedding photograph on the mantel. This would be the first time she had a man in her apartment other than co-workers. It felt weird as if in a strange way she was cheating on her husband. Victory shook the thought from her mind, knowing she was being too hard on herself.

She pointed toward the kitchen. "Have a seat. I'll be back in a minute. My daughter's home from college. I don't want to wake her."

As Derrick walked by, he asked, "How old is your daughter?"

"Twenty-three going on forty."

"Sounds like fun."

"Do you have kids?"

He shook his head. "No. And I've never been married either."

She found it odd that an extremely attractive man in his mid-forties who ran a successful gaming company would be single. Her investigative skills kicked in. "Why is that?"

"I suppose, always being too busy with work. And the fact I've never met the right person. What about you?"

For a moment, she wasn't sure what to say, the truth at times still too painful to say. "I was married. Josh died last year."

Uncomfortable silence pulsed through the air.

"I'm sorry."

Victory watched Derrick set breakfast on the table. "Be right back." She walked down the hallway to the spare bedroom, opened the door, and poked her head inside.

The blinds were open. Sunlight splashed across the bed and floor.

The bed was still made the way Victory had made it before Jade had come home.

The hair on the back of her neck prickled. She walked inside the room and noticed a note on the corner of the dresser. She picked up the paper and read the message.

Meeting some friends at Ultra Club 51 for a few hours. Love J.

With two serial killers roaming the streets, Victory tried to squash the panic rising in her chest. She looked at the bed. Jade hadn't been home all night. She clutched the note in her hand and went back to the kitchen, telling herself to stay calm.

"Something wrong?" Derrick handed her a coffee.

Victory took the coffee and sat down at the table, placing the note beside her. "I don't know. Jade. She didn't come home last night. It's not something my daughter would normally do." She wasn't sure why she was telling this to a man she barely knew, and one she was suspicious of.

His gaze moved to the note, then back to her. "Maybe she's staying at a friend's house."

Her stomach tightened, signaling something wasn't right. Her motherly instincts were always spot on, always had been. Victory grabbed her phone from the table and typed a text message and sent it to her daughter. Then she sent a message to Rebecca and Marley, two of Jade's closest friends.

"I'm sure she's fine," Derrick said.

Victory wanted to believe him. She took a drink of

coffee and observed her hand trembling slightly.

Derrick reached across the table and touched her hand. "You're shaking."

The same familiarity of his touch that Victory had experienced in his office when they first met, spiked through her. She moved her hand away and set down her coffee.

"It must be tough being a mother, and an FBI agent."

"At times it is. All the horrible things I've seen throughout my career are always in the back of my mind. All I want to do is protect my kid from the evil in the world." Her phone beeped.

Derrick smiled. "Maybe that's her."

Victory seized the phone and checked the display. Her heart felt as if it had stopped as she read the text message from Rebecca.

Jade left the club before we did
Have her call me when she gets up

She sent another message.

Is Marley at home or with you?

A few seconds passed, and Victory's phone beeped again.

She slept over at my place last night. Something wrong?

Déjà vu hit Victory, like a punch in the gut. Her hand shook as she clutched the phone. She contemplated answering the message but changed her mind. Panic, dark, and threatening surged through her as images of The Wrapper's victims looped through her mind like a horror movie.

She looked up at Derrick. "I need to go to the club."

Derrick stood. Lines crept across his forehead. "I'll drive you. You're trembling like crazy."

She nodded, realizing even her head was shaking.

As Victory put on her coat and boots, a dozen scenarios raced through her mind. She kept coming back to one. What if Jeremy Elder had taken Jade because the FBI had gotten too close? Because *she* had gotten too close?

For the first time since Josh had died, Victory prayed to God she was wrong.

✻ ✻ ✻

As Derrick sped the SUV down McMillian Street, tree branches along the road appeared bent, twisted out of shape under the weight of the snow. He was happy he had the reporter's laptop, but things could still blow up for everyone involved with the Elara Project. They still had no idea who had leaked the information to Melissa Mann. He tried not to think about it, at least for now.

Victory sat next to him, talking on her phone. She'd made call after call, looking for her daughter, with no success. Derrick was worried too. From what she'd told him about The Wrapper, considering his own line of work, he was even horrified. He hoped she was wrong about the serial killer and Jade had spent the night with another friend, someone Victory didn't know about. A new boyfriend, perhaps.

She ended a call and quietly peered out the side window.

"Any luck?" Derrick asked.

"Luck is nothing more than the imaginary line between disaster and survival. I've experienced it, dealt with it." Victory continued to stare out the window.

Derrick couldn't imagine what she was feeling right now, not knowing where her daughter was. He clutched the steering wheel and turned into the club's large empty lot and parked. He spotted her partner leaning against his vehicle next to the three-storey gray vinyl-sided building.

Victory opened the door and high-tailed it to Ryan.

Derrick killed the engine and sat for a moment, then got out and followed her. It was colder than he had expected. He glanced at the dull, gray sky. It seemed almost menacing, somehow. Bitter cold air brushed against his face and stung his skin.

"How you holding up, Vic?" Ryan asked, his voice overflowing with concern.

"I don't know. I've contacted everyone Jade knows and no one has seen or heard from her. I'm afraid he has her, Ryan. We have to find her."

Derrick caught the emotion in her voice, the way her voice quivered, and her tone changed.

"Let's not jump to conclusions. Sean's at your place checking the apartment building's security footage and any other cameras in the area." Ryan looked over her shoulder and glanced at Derrick. "What's he doing here?"

"It's a long story."

"But—"

Victory stiffened and held up her hand to stop him. "This isn't the time. Can you get a hold of the club's owner and get him over here right away? I need access to the cameras."

Derrick heard her voice come out firm and steady, considering the stress she was under.

"I'll get on it." Ryan put his hand on her shoulder. "We're going to find her, Vic." He stared at Derrick briefly and pulled out his phone and walked away.

She turned to Derrick. "Sorry. He can be intense at times. He means well."

"It's okay. I understand. Emotions are running high."

Ryan walked toward them and stopped beside Victory. "The owner of the club will be here in a couple of minutes. He lives pretty close."

"Okay." Victory's voice and gaze drifted away.

Derrick could tell she was deep in thought the way she was staring at one of the cameras aimed at the parking lot. He noticed something else, something dark and personal—fear in the back of her eyes.

✳   ✳   ✳

On the third floor of the club, Victory stood inside a spacious storage room, her eyes glued to video footage of the dance floor. Ryan was next to her, going through the video from the parking lot while Derrick had slipped out to get them coffee.

Victory's phone buzzed. She yanked the phone from her pocket with break-neck speed.

"Sean, any news?"

"I've got a screen grab from a camera across the street from your apartment. A blue Toyota Camry. I'm sending you the photo now."

Her phone beeped. She checked the message. A grainy photograph filled the screen. The air swooshed out of her lungs.

Jeremy Elder.

Her legs turned to mush, about to give out. She fought through it, steadying herself against a metal shelf, knowing the only way to help her daughter was to remain strong even though Victory was dying inside. She'd lost Josh. She couldn't lose Jade too.

"Vic?" Sean asked. "You still there?"

"Yeah."

"It looks like he was parked there for quite a while, watching your building. We ran the plate. It's registered to Betsy Elder, his dead mother..."

Sean continued to speak but Victory had already tuned out. Her greatest fear had come true. The Wrapper had Jade.

At the same moment, Victory's mind deserted her. She screamed silently into blackness and the blackness screamed back. Sanity seemed to flee. She envisioned herself as a wild animal, pouncing on Elder, slicing and ripping his flesh with sharp claws and teeth. Then something interrupted her. It was reason. Cold, hard logic. It dragged her back and held her firmly, making her understand that her child needed her. She must remain calm, and sane, and focused on what she needed to do. Victory knew she needed to push her raw emotion aside the best she could, just as years of training and experience had taught her. She had to maintain a professional detachment for Jade's sake, no matter how difficult. She forced herself to focus.

"...couple of my CIs are working the streets and a dozen guys from patrol," Sean said.

"Alright, Sean."

Victory lowered the phone, the panic returning, her lungs tight. Her heart thumped. She couldn't breathe. She gasped, then let out a sharp breath. Her eyes met Ryan's and she passed the phone to him. "Elder was parked outside my apartment building last night."

Ryan's eyes widened. He took the phone and looked

at the image then looked up at her. "Christ. That's him."

A beat of tense silence filled the space.

Her mind flooded again with images of The Wrapper's victims, vivid and cruel.

Another body would turn up.

The contents of her stomach surged up the back of her throat. Victory snatched a small plastic wastebasket from the floor and threw up in it as Derrick returned with coffee for them.

Derrick handed Ryan a coffee. "Is she okay? She looks really pale."

"I'm right here. I can hear what you're saying."

Ryan shook his head and exchanged glances with Victory. "The Wrapper has Jade."

Derrick frowned and set the other coffee cup down next to one of the monitors. He touched her wrist gently in a comforting way. "What can I do to help?"

"Unless you can find Jade, there isn't much you can do," Victory said, her gaze lingering on his face, hating to have to say the horrible truth out loud.

"I have a helicopter. Money. Anything. Whatever you need."

Victory appreciated the offer from a man she barely knew. But there was nothing Derrick could do to help find her daughter.

"How did he know where you lived?" Ryan's eyes shifted to Derrick.

Her mind churned, searching for the answer. When she found the answer, it hit her hard. "Oh, God." Her stomach gurgled, and her shoulders slumped. "Jade had strep throat last year during spring break. I picked up a prescription for her at CenterTown Pharmacy because Walgreens was too busy. I'd completely forgotten about it." Victory wrapped her arm around her stomach and fought from vomiting again.

"He had your address on file," Derrick said.

Wetness broke out along Victory's hairline and an odd coldness settled between her shoulder blades. The room suddenly felt too small. The walls closed in around her. "I need to get some air."

She rushed out of the room and raced down the stairs, taking two steps at a time. On the main floor, she skidded to a stop at the back of the club and shoved the door open with her shoulder.

Snow fell, hushed, and heavy and covered the ground with a fresh layer of white. Chilly air burst into her lungs. She stood there, her legs weak, taking in gulps of air and letting them out, trying to calm her nerves. She had no idea where the killer was or where he'd taken Jade. The thought horrified her. Guilt stabbed at her heart and she cursed to herself. She fought off the feelings.

Soft footsteps approached from behind. Victory glanced over her shoulder at Derrick.

"Just checking to make sure you're okay."

She looked at him then back outside. "I don't think I'll ever be okay. This is my fault. If I hadn't used that pharmacy—"

"It isn't your fault. I'm sure this is the last thing you ever thought would happen."

"I don't know how to find her. We don't have any leads other than Elder was in one specific area at some point. I've got squat."

"Ryan's still looking through the video. Maybe something will turn up that's helpful."

Victory knew Derrick didn't understand what The Wrapper did to his victims. But she did. "He burns them alive." A tear escaped from the corner of her eye. She blinked it away and had a tough time getting the words out. "From everything I've learned about Jeremy Elder, there's a good chance Jade isn't going to make it unless I can find her before the end of the day."

CHAPTER THIRTEEN

Derrick had a dilemma. He couldn't walk away, knowing he had the ability to help Victory find her daughter. He'd been watching Victory and her partner search the club's security footage for the last two hours. His phone vibrated in his pocket. He pulled it out and checked the message. It was from his father.

Have you checked the reporter's laptop?

He quickly typed a message.

Not yet. Get back to you in a few hours.

He hit send and slipped the phone back into his pocket.

"That's Jade right there at the bar." Victory pointed to a young woman on the monitor's screen.

Jade looked a lot like her mother. Very pretty. She had the same long red hair and blue eyes.

Ryan pointed to two young women on the dance floor, dancing with two guys. "Is that Marley and Re-

DEADLY SHADOW | 163

Victory nodded slowly and kept her gaze glued to the screen. "They left Jade alone."

The anguish in her voice was undeniable. Derrick felt bad that he couldn't help her. If he did, it would put the Elara Project at risk. His gut clenched.

"Right there." Ryan's finger moved to the lower portion of the screen. "There's Elder. He's heading to the bar." Derrick watched Jade turn her head and look toward the dance floor at her friends. Behind her, the bartender was hunched over a box on the floor pulling out bottles of liquor and stocking the shelf above him, while a female bartender was busy with a dozen customers at the other end of the bar. The killer slid up beside Jade when she wasn't looking. He moved his hand to her glass. It looked like he put something in her drink.

Victory blew out a shaky breath. "He spiked her drink with the Rohypnol."

"Then he probably played the knight in shining armor and offered her a ride home. She'd be too out of it to say no." Ryan hit pause and looked at Victory. "You sure you want to keep watching? I can go through the rest. You don't have to do this."

"No." A line formed between her eyebrows." I need to know what happened. Everything." Victory pressed the 'play' button.

For a long while, she said nothing, her eyes transfixed on the monitor's screen.

Derrick felt helpless watching her. The same helplessness he'd once felt as a child after he'd cracked Jake's skull with a rock.

"That's all there is," Victory said.

Ryan hit the 'stop' button. "We know she got into his

car. They turned out of the parking lot and headed west toward Mill Creek. Not much to go on. It's a lead at least."

"They could be anywhere. See what we can get from the traffic cams in the area. Maybe we can narrow down his location."

Ryan left the room to make the call in the hallway.

After he left, Victory glanced at Derrick. The tense set of her mouth loosened a bit.

"You know, you don't have to stay. I'm sure you have other things to do. I never got the chance to thank you for breakfast, not that I had the chance to enjoy it."

He smiled. "Next time. I don't mind being here. My work allows me the freedom to spend my time the way I want. I wish there was something I could do to help you find Jade."

The room fell quiet.

"What I need is a miracle."

"If you don't mind me asking, what happened to him, your husband?" Derrick asked.

Sadness clouded her features, particularly her eyes.

"He tried to stop a bank robber from harming anyone. It didn't work out too well."

"I am sorry. Was he an FBI agent too?"

"No. It's because of me that Jade lost her father."

"How so?"

"Josh was at the bank because of me. I'd forgotten to make a deposit that couldn't wait. He didn't know the bank was being robbed when he went in. It cost him his life."

"That's a heavy burden to be carrying. Your husband's death wasn't your fault, just like what's happening with Jade isn't either."

She swallowed hard. "It feels that way at times."

He studied her for a moment, the vulnerability returning. There was such pain in the back of her eyes. A miracle was exactly what Derrick could provide. He wasn't sure if he could live with himself if he did nothing. He could use his paranormal skills to find Jeremy Elder and maybe save Jade. The cost could be great no matter what he decided to do. He'd be exposing the project, himself, not to mention his father and the president.

Ryan returned and stopped in the doorway. "Our team finished processing Elder's Acura."

"What did they find?" Victory asked.

"Hair, skin, and blood probably belonging to multiple victims. Just waiting for the DNA results to confirm. And Sean called."

Her eyes widened. "News about Jade?"

"Sorry, Vic. Nothing yet. He wanted you to know forensics didn't turn up any evidence at Melissa Mann's house. Not a single fingerprint belonging to anyone besides herself. Pretty weird scene. Things aren't adding up, just like the Bullington case. The Shadow might be involved."

Derrick's pulse jumped at the mention of The Shadow.

"What if Melissa had dug up dirt on The Shadow too? What if she had learned his identity, was about to out him? The tech guys are going through her laptop, right?" Victory asked.

"That's the thing, Vic. The laptop made it to the CPDs evidence locker. The Paper trail confirms it was logged in. It's not there."

"The laptop is missing?"

Ryan nodded. "It's vanished."

Derrick was grateful he'd gotten the reporter's laptop when he did. Victory was thinking hard about the news.

"Someone doesn't want us to know what's on her laptop," she said. "Someone with enough power to have it disappear from a police evidence locker."

At the same time, Derrick's phone vibrated again. He pulled it out. "Sorry, I need to take this." He ducked out into the hallway and walked far enough away from prying ears.

"What is it, Dad? I'm kind of busy right now." His gaze shifted down the stairs then back to the storage room.

"The president's worried."

"Why?" Derrick lowered his voice. "He shouldn't be. We've got the laptop."

"The source, son. Whoever gave the information to the reporter about the Elara Project is still out there. We don't know what they plan on doing with it."

"I'll finish up here and call you if I find something on her laptop." He disconnected.

Any anxiety and guilt Derrick had experienced after eliminating the reporter rippled through him again when he headed back to the storage room and heard Ryan say, "They're going through her cell phone records right now."

Sweat broke out across Derrick's forehead and his scalp tingled. He knew the reporter had never called him like he'd told Victory. Melissa was already dead. Victory would learn he had lied when the phone records were examined. He stood outside the door for a moment to gather himself.

"I'm terrified I'm going to lose Jade. I can't. I should be doing more to find her."

"Vic, you're doing everything you can other than driving around looking for her. We know that's not going to help find her. We need a good lead."

"He's going to kill her, Ryan. We both know how this works."

Derrick heard absolute agony in Victory's voice. Guilt plagued him. He cursed under his breath. He had to help Victory. He might be Jade's only hope.

* * *

After Derrick arrived home at twelve-thirty, he sat behind his desk in his office at the far end of the house. He opened Melissa's laptop and waited for it to boot up. When it was ready, he typed 'Elara Project' into the computer's search box and hit enter. Seconds passed with no results.

Thirty minutes later, he still hadn't found anything related to the project. He gritted his teeth and kept searching through the document folders, his mind wandering to Victory. He wondered if she had any news about Jade. Derrick hoped it wasn't too late for her daughter.

He planned on helping Victory, but he needed to get this task out of the way to satisfy his father and President Burke. He understood both situations were critical. He had to choose which task took priority. Unfortunately, this one did, to keep them all out of jail and avoid exposing a shocking new reality to America, and the world. Derrick took a drink of his scotch and had a sinking feeling in his gut.

Another hour flew by and he finally hit the jackpot. He'd found the reporter's notes, saved under the file name 'govcovup.doc'. Derrick let out a breath of relief and began reading the contents. Halfway through, his jaw dropped open when he recognized a name. It was the original source.

Shane Beckham.

Derrick couldn't believe it. Shane was one of the enlistees, a month after Derrick had been recruited. The guy had quit six months in. He kept reading.

Met with Shane Beckham...November 1...at his house...

According to the notes, Melissa had met with Shane eight times in the past three weeks. The reporter knew almost everything including that the project had been sanctioned by President Burke, and many presidents before him dating back to the Cold War. Derrick finished reading, leaned back in the chair, and closed his eyes. His father wouldn't be pleased.

They couldn't have recruits blabbing about the project. This was a problem. A huge problem that needed to be dealt with immediately. The issue couldn't be put off until tonight when the man was sleeping.

Derrick knew Shane's gift was visual mind reading. He could see the thoughts of people as images, and if they'd been present during certain events. His special ability had been used on the ground in terrorist states, Iran and Syria, and helped eliminate dozens of known terrorists, in turn, protecting the United States from future attacks. He'd also helped track down a CIA mole. Derrick couldn't imagine having the ability. The constant visuals would become draining over time. He had no idea why Shane had decided to play the whistleblower game, putting everyone and the Elara Project at risk. The problem needed to be looked after.

He grabbed his phone on the desk and dialed Evelyn's number. After a few rings, the woman answered.

"Hello?"

"Hi, Evelyn. It's Derrick."

"It's good to hear from you. What can I do for you?"

"Do you remember Shane Beckham?"

"Of course. He was the oldest in the group, a visual mind reader. Our first, and only one. Nice man."

"Do you happen to have his address on file? I thought I'd try to reconnect with some of the old recruits." He didn't want Evelyn involved any more than she already was. Her name was in Melissa's file, along with the colonel's.

"I think so. Give me a second to check the system."

A few minutes passed before she came back on the line.

"1631 Wold Avenue. I don't know if he still lives there, though. It's been a long time."

He tore off the corner of his desk calendar and jotted down the address. "Thanks, Evelyn. I'll check it out."

"Don't be a stranger, Derrick. The recruits would love the chance to hang out with you. Nathan thought you were pretty cool."

"He's amazing. I'll free up some time next week and stop by."

"Great. Looking forward to it. You and I have a lot of catching up to do."

"Thanks again, Evelyn. We'll talk next week."

Derrick put the phone down and shoved the address in his pocket. He glanced at his watch. 2:30 p.m. Everything came at a cost. He picked up his phone again and called his father.

❊   ❊   ❊

Derrick parked across the street from the three-storey house. It was majestic, with its massive white pillars, huge windows, and slate-colored shutters. If Shane lived here, he'd done well for himself. The house was one of many multi-million-dollar homes in the East Walnut Hills neighborhood.

He exited the SUV and walked to the other side of the street. The sun poked through the dismal soot-colored clouds as snowflakes fluttered in the late afternoon air.

His father was dismayed to learn that Shane was Melissa Mann's source. So was Derrick. He knew the guy had left the project claiming he couldn't handle the emotional fallout that came with killing a target. Whether it was the truth or not, Derrick knew what he needed to do. He rang the doorbell. Seconds later, the door opened.

The man looked different than Derrick remembered. He was about the same height as Derrick. His brown hair was clipped short around his ears in a military cut. He was bulked up. Even his face was beefy compared to the last time Derrick had seen him. The muscles in his arms flexed through the long-sleeved shirt he was wearing.

"Derrick?" Shane poked his head outside the door and glanced up and down the street. "What are you doing here?"

"I thought it would be great to reconnect with some of the old recruits. I took the chance your address hadn't changed. Nice house."

"I inherited it when my father died a year after I left the Elara Project. It's been in our family home since the 1920s."

"Great architecture," Derrick said.

"Come on in."

After Derrick took off his boots and coat, Shane led him into a large great room with a gas fireplace and floor-to-ceiling windows. The spacious room resembled an old stone structure complete with wood beams and soaring ceilings.

Derrick took a seat on one of the couches directly across from Shane. "What have you been up to since you left the project?"

A weird, silent awkwardness filled the air. Derrick could tell the man was trying to read his mind.

"I've been working for a Blackwater-type private military security company. More my style than reading minds."

"That's great. You must be out of the country quite a bit."

Shane nodded. "I've read that you've done well with your gaming company."

"I have." Derrick looked around the room for any signs that they weren't the only ones in the house. "Married?"

"Yeah. My wife, Carla, works at the same security company. She's out of the country, working in Iraq since you want to know so badly."

Shane had read his mind. Derrick needed to get to the point, and then do what was necessary. It would take every ounce of his energy to eliminate the man.

"I know you were in contact with Melissa Mann about the Elara Project. Why would expose the project, expose us?"

Shane looked at Derrick. "I'm not like you just because I can read minds. The project needs to be shut down, should have been canned decades ago. When I started working for Northridge International, I realized I was actually helping people and assisting countries in turmoil. That's how we protect our own country—not by using paranormal skills to take out whoever we want. Because of the Elara Project's actions, many of the countries I work in are now in worse shape and are even more dangerous to the US."

Derrick studied him. He'd heard a lot about Northridge International, run by former special ops personnel, mainly Delta Force soldiers. The private military company provided security and mission support on the ground as well as logistical support. He'd also heard the group had been heavily involved with the Iraq War.

"Come on, man. We're both doing the same thing, just differently. The Elara Project isn't going anywhere."

Life flickered behind Shane's eyes. Surprise stung his face. As much as Derrick had tried to block out his thoughts about what he was going to do to the man, Shane's paranormal abilities were too strong. He knew what was coming.

Derrick's body stiffened as he directed his energy at the man's arms.

A spark of energy jolted Shane to his feet. He tried to stop his arms from lifting toward his head. "Please don't do this."

Derrick ignored him. He kept staring and concentrating.

Shane's hands shook violently, out of control as if he was an electrocuted string puppet, then bucked around both sides of his neck. They stayed there. He smacked into an end table with his knees, knocking it over.

Sweat ran down Derrick's face and dripped off his chin. He grunted against the man's physical strength until Shane's hands were firmly wrapped around his own neck. Derrick focused.

The man's fingers clawed at his skin then both hands squeezed. His green eyes bulged. He gulped for air as he fought to stop from strangling himself. The skin on his face turned white, then gray, then a deathly shade of bluish-gray. His legs buckled. He dropped to the floor and rolled onto his back.

Derrick worked his energy harder, his body trembling uncontrollably.

Minutes later, Shane was dead.

* * *

The last remnants of daylight extinguished below the horizon as evening settled over the city. It was snowing again. At five-thirty, Victory stood in front of her living room window and watched people on the street below, going about their lives.

Jade was her world, all she had left from twenty years of marriage. Victory had spent the last two hours searching neighborhoods that intersected with Elder's house and many of his victims, handing out missing flyers about Jade, speaking with business owners, anyone who would listen to her. Then common sense kicked in. She knew the chances of finding her daughter by scouring the streets without a lead was nothing more than a wild goose chase. Her stomach knotted into a tight ball as she grappled with the anger and anguish. All she could do was wait, each ticking minute feeling like ten lifetimes.

Another piece of her died when she'd learned The Wrapper had taken Jade. She wished Josh was here, to comfort, reassure her that everything was going to be okay. She took a gulp of her beer then picked up the remote from the coffee table and turned on the TV to help with the drone of silence since she'd arrived home. After finding her usual twenty-four-hour news station, she turned the volume on low and tossed the remote on the couch.

Afterward, she wandered into the kitchen and opened the fridge door, glanced at the contents, then closed it. She couldn't eat. Her appetite had evaporated hours ago.

Ryan was at the office, working with Curtis and three other agents, hoping to get a lead on Jade's whereabouts. Sean was meeting with his informants every hour and checking in with the CPD officers pounding the streets. Everyone was doing what they could to find Jade. Victory had to figure out where Elder had taken her daughter. For the second time in almost a year, helplessness washed over her. She had no clue where he'd take her daughter.

Victory pulled out a chair and sat. Her eyes moved to the accordion folder at the end of the table containing The Shadow case, the last thing she was worried about. She rested her elbows on the table. Then her thoughts turned briefly to Derrick.

She didn't usually share information about her personal life with anyone, only occasionally with Ryan. She wasn't sure why she'd let Derrick into her life on somewhat of a personal level. It was out of character. It was the circumstances, she told herself, the truth harder to accept. She liked him. She was drawn to him, the mystery, the intensity, and was interested in knowing what he was hiding.

Her phone rang. She grabbed it off the table. "Have

you got anything?"

"Maybe," Ryan said. "Curtis and I went back and looked at The Wrapper's first three kills. I know we've gone through them a hundred times, but we noticed a notation from forensics. It might not mean anything. Or it might mean something."

"What is it?"

"Trace amounts of a low-foam detergent floor cleaner used for cleaning car parts like gaskets and seals. It was found on Justine Walker's left palm."

A tinge of hope flowed through her body. At least it was a possible clue. "Justine was his second Cincinnati victim."

"We're heading out in a few minutes to search abandoned warehouses, ones that once housed or manufactured car parts. We've got it narrowed down to nine within the vicinity of his home, and the pharmacy that coincides with the parks where he dumped his victims."

Her breathing quickened, and her chest felt heavy. "He could have taken her to Cleveland." She paused, taking what she could get at this point. "It's worth a try. Pick me up. I'm coming with you."

Piercing silence filled the other end of the line.

"Sorry, Vic. Curtis wants you to stand down. So does Joe Mains. A direct order from the top. You're too close to the case."

"Are you kidding me? Damn right I'm too close." Her voice turned louder, angrier. "That's my kid out there, not theirs."

"I know. Don't shoot the messenger. Hang in there. Do what they want for now, okay? I'll call you in a bit."

She slammed the phone down on the table without saying goodbye and heard a knock at the door over the electrical hum coming from the fridge.

Victory went to the door and peered through the peephole. *Derrick?* For a second, she'd thought about not answering the door, then changed her mind. She unlocked and opened the door.

Derrick flashed her a million-dollar smile. "I think I can find your daughter."

✻　✻　✻

Derrick spotted suspicion in Victory's eyes. She wasn't buying it. After a few minutes, she let him in and headed to the kitchen. He followed her, nervous and concerned. He was about to put everything on the line. The Elara Project, his father, the president, to help locate her daughter. His eyes shifted to her holster, to her gun.

She opened the fridge and pulled out a beer and handed it to him. "How can you find Jade when no one else can?"

Derrick took the bottle of beer, unsure where to start. He set the drink on the kitchen island. He'd need something stronger after this conversation.

"I can find her but it's going to cost."

She shook her head and laughed. "You want me to pay you to find my daughter? What kind of scam are you running?"

"It isn't a scam. I meant something different. Not money. I want, I need, something in return."

She stared at him. Confusion crossed her face.

"I don't have time for games." She walked past him, brushing against his shoulder. "I think you should leave."

He grabbed her arm and stopped her in mid-step. "I'm not playing games." His tone turned stern. "Do you

DEADLY SHADOW | 177

want to find Jade?"

"Of course, I do. How dare you even ask."

"I *can* find her." Derrick released her arm, convinced he finally had her full attention. Victory went to the other side of the table. Her eyes met his.

He inhaled a silent deep breath and let it out. "I need a couple of assurances. One. What I am about to tell you will never be revealed to anyone. Ever."

She nodded slowly in agreement, not knowing what she was agreeing to.

"Secondly, protection for my own sins."

"O—kay. I don't know what you're talking about but if you can really find Jade, then I couldn't care less what sins you're talking about or have committed. I need to find my daughter. If you can help, then help, please, before it's too late. Elder will kill her."

His heart pounded. Anxiety sped through his veins, making his muscles feel tight and hard. He looked at the floor then up at Victory, trying to find all the right words. "I have special paranormal skills. I've had them all my life, as long as I can remember."

Her eyes widened and lit up. "Like ESP or something?"

"No." He hesitated. "Etheric travel. Meaning I'm able to move in real time, observing people while my body is asleep. I can connect with the killer, find out where he is."

Victory didn't say anything, clearly absorbing what he had said.

"I also can move objects with my mind. It's called psychokinesis."

She remained silent for a long time, adding things up, connecting the dots. Derrick could see it, feel it. She knew who he was.

The blood drained from her face.

With lightning speed Victory yanked the gun out of her holster. She aimed the barrel at his forehead. "You're —The Shadow. You killed Eddie Bullington, Steven Rothwell, the —"

"I'm a government assassin."

"An assassin? You're a cold-blooded killer."

He walked toward her slowly, cautiously, keeping his eyes on the weapon. He noticed her fingers tighten around the handle of the gun.

"Don't move."

Derrick stopped, worried she might shoot him. "Put the gun away, Victory. You don't need it. What I've told you is all true. I am a government assassin. It's my job. What I've done doesn't matter. Think of Jade. Think about getting your daughter back."

She jabbed the weapon at him. "I said don't move. It matters to me. Extortion is a criminal offense. I'm taking you in. It's *my* job."

Derrick narrowed his eyes and looked at the gun, focusing all his energy at her hand. Her fingers twitched, and raised, starting to loosen around the gun. Victory's face went slack, her mouth open, as she stared wide-eyed in shock, fighting against his energy with all her strength. He kept directing all his energy until her grip slackened completely.

The gun slingshotted across the table into his hand.

He two-handed the weapon and turned the gun on Victory. "I know you want to save Jade. Accept my terms. Time is running out. You know that. I want to help. I really do."

She took a step back, shaking her head. Then a look of recognition on her face.

"You killed Melissa." Her gaze darted to the phone on the table, an arm's length away.

"Yes." His eyes wandered to the phone. Derrick trained his energy on the cell phone. It slid to his end of the table, out of Victory's reach.

"You bastard."

Derrick understood her anger. He'd been able to dodge her, and the FBI, for two decades. The realization that he was The Shadow, the killer she'd been seeking for so long, was a hard one for Victory to swallow.

"We can stay like this for as long as you want. Or you can agree to the terms, then we can discuss finding Jade. It's your choice, Victory."

He hated the way he'd been forced to deal with her, so tough, a bully, sounding so uncaring. He liked her. That much was true. He could see the hurt in her eyes. He'd betrayed her. He had to, to save her daughter. Victory would understand one day. At least Derrick hoped she would.

Ten minutes passed, and Derrick wondered how much longer the woman was going to hold out and stand her ground. Finally, Victory pulled out a chair and sat.

"You've given me no choice. I accept your terms."

Derrick searched Victory's face to ensure she was telling the truth. When he was confident she was, he lowered the weapon and released the magazine onto the table. He set the Glock beside him, convinced she probably had more ammunition hidden somewhere in the apartment.

"I didn't want to do it like this. I want you to know that. I didn't have much of a choice. I'm in a difficult position. There are others involved. I'm putting them at risk, putting everything at risk. You have no idea."

"You're a killer."

The truth was hard for him to hear, to accept, the way she said it with such disdain. He eliminated targets to protect his country, something Victory may never understand.

"I was twenty-one when I was recruited into the Elara Project, a covert government program utilizing people with special paranormal abilities to help defend the security of the United States. The project dates back to shortly after the end of World War II."

"There are more like you?"

"A few. Each of the recruits have different paranormal skills."

"Like what?"

Derrick didn't want to get into too many details. He was sure the truth was already tough enough for her to believe. "Mind readers, remote viewers."

"President Burke sanctioned the project, knowing he was signing death warrants?"

He noted nervousness in Victory's voice as she spoke. She was scared of him. That wasn't the way Derrick wanted things to be.

He nodded. "Yes, the project was sanctioned by the president and many before him. You have to understand —"

"I don't have to understand anything. Who else is involved?"

Derrick paused for a moment before speaking. "My father."

CHAPTER FOURTEEN

Victory couldn't believe what she had just witnessed. She downed half of her beer in one swallow. She felt as if she'd been sucked into watching a special effects show. The gun. Derrick had removed it from her hand with ease using only his mind. How was that possible? Yet she'd seen it with her own eyes. Then the weapon was in his hand, pointed at her.

Victory never believed in anything paranormal, and especially not people having strange, inexplicable abilities. Now she was fully aware of the secret Derrick had been hiding. He was an assassin on the government's payroll. She honestly didn't know who she could trust. Could she even trust Derrick to find Jade? She downed the rest of her beer, desperately needing another, but had to keep her mind clear to find her daughter.

Victory was floored by the revelation the Secretary of Defense and President Burke were involved. She was an FBI agent. She'd taken an oath to defend the Constitution of the United States against all enemies, foreign and domestic.

She didn't know how she was going to live with herself, knowing Derrick had killed so many people. The victim's families deserved closure. Victory doubted Eddie Bullington and Melissa Mann were killed to protect the country. There was more to the story.

"Why did you kill Bullington and Melissa?"

"Melissa had uncovered the truth about the Elara Project from a past recruit. She and Bullington were going to go public about the project. If they had, lives would be in danger."

"You murdered them to shut them up."

"I don't see it that way. The fallout would have been costly if the public knew what was going on."

"Costly? Like you and your father being arrested? And the president?"

Derrick's mouth twisted. "What we've accomplished through the Elara Project outweighs what I've had to do over the years. We've been able to stop dozens of foreign and domestic terrorist attacks, taking out some very bad guys, saving lives. It's an important project. The country needs it."

She frowned at his so-called logic. "Keep telling yourself that. The people you killed had kids. You've destroyed families. How can you live with that? Now you're forcing me to keep your dirty secret, and if I don't, after you find Jade?"

He took a drink of the whiskey she had poured for him, then set the glass down. "You don't want to cross me, Victory. I have the ability to kill you at any time to ensure my secret remains buried. You've seen what I can do."

His eyes gleamed. He was dead serious.

A shiver rocketed through her as another realization slammed her. "It was you—in Bullington's house. And you were in my bedroom when I thought I was dreaming."

"Yes."

"Why?"

Her phone rang.

Derrick glanced at the phone, and then at her. Their gazes locked. "Remember what you agreed to." He shoved the phone down the table to her.

She picked up the phone and answered it. "Please tell me you have something, Ryan?"

"We've searched four warehouses, so far nothing. How are you holding up?"

"I'm not." Her own words flashed through her mind.

"The anniversary is important to him, means everything to him. He has to kill even if it means he'll get caught or killed."

"Have faith, Vic. It's all we've got right now. Sean and a couple of local cops are heading to some of the other warehouses on the list to make the searches go quicker. I know we're on the clock."

Victory glanced at Derrick. Sweat lined his upper lip. "I'm checking into a lead on my end. I'll let you know if it pans out."

"Curtis will be pissed if he finds out you're working behind the scenes."

"He's been angry all his life. Just don't tell him. I'll deal with him when I have to. Call me if you find anything." She placed the phone down.

Fear pulsed through her. She wanted her daughter home. Victory wasn't completely convinced Derrick could find her. She wanted more than anything to believe he could.

Victory leaned back in the chair and crossed her arms over her chest. She glared at Derrick. "Now what?"

"Tell me everything you know about Jeremy Elder."

✽   ✽   ✽

Inside the warehouse, Jeremy sat in his car and went through the woman's purse. He dumped the contents on his lap and opened her wallet. He found her driver's license tucked into one of the compartments along with fifty dollars. He threw the money on the dash and examined the ID. His eyes drifted to the cage where Jade was asleep on the bare mattress completely out of it from the Rohypnol he'd spiked her drink with.

She was pretty, but certainly not his type. Jade didn't look anything like Lily. He hoped she would come too soon. He needed her alert to experience his wrath.

The FBI agent should have minded her own business. If he was going down, then Agent McClane deserved to lose something dear to her the way he'd lost Lily. He still couldn't figure out where he had screwed up. He'd been so careful not to leave a trace of evidence on any of the women.

Something happened. Something he'd missed.

He tossed Jade's purse on the passenger seat and climbed out of the vehicle. It wouldn't be much longer before the woman was awake. He couldn't wait.

✽   ✽   ✽

After Victory finished telling Derrick everything she knew about Jeremy Elder, she paced in front of the dining room table, clutching her cell phone. It was ten-fifteen and she knew Elder usually killed his victims between midnight and three in the morning.

Time wasn't on their side.

As painful as it was, she had succumbed to the realization that he may have already killed Jade. The thought bit at her soul. She had to hang onto every ounce of hope she had, and even that was fading by the minute.

Derrick was in the bedroom asleep in her bed. He continued to claim he could do the impossible: connect with the killer. At this point, she didn't have a choice but to believe him.

Her phone vibrated. She kept her voice low, not to disturb Derrick. "Ryan. Anything?"

"Nothing. We still have three more warehouses to check. We've got a lot of boots on the ground, canvassing the areas where we think Elder may have taken Jade. But things aren't looking good, Vic."

She didn't want to say it aloud because then it would be real. But it was the grim reality. Her voice faltered. "I—know."

"Anything happening with your lead?" Ryan asked.

She glanced at the hallway toward her bedroom and fought to find her voice. "Not yet. I'll let you know. Keep looking, Ryan. We can't give up. We can't let Jade down. I can't let her down."

"We're not going to give up. Not until she's home."

Victory ended the call and put the phone down on the table. The phone vibrated, and she scooped the phone up again. "Sean. Did you—"

"Just hang on, Vic."

There was a lengthy pause on the other end.

She kept pacing.

"We've got something. One sec."

A chill blasted through her. Victory held her breath, bracing for possible bad news. She heard voices in the background. She wanted to scream, "Hurry up!".

"We just located Jade's cell phone," Sean said.

She let out the breath she was holding. There was still hope. "Where?"

"In a snowbank about four miles west of your apartment."

"What about traffic cams?"

"We lost his vehicle about three miles out. Several cameras around the city have gone down due to the high winds. There's a massive storm blowing in."

Reality hit. Her heart sank for the hundredth time. "Keep me posted." She disconnected and tromped down the new round of anxiety.

Elder had discarded Jade's cell phone much like his victims. He wasn't stupid. He knew exactly what he was doing. The man savored power. He hadn't taken Jade to use as leverage. He had taken her for revenge. He planned on killing her—if he hadn't already.

In the bedroom, Victory sat in the chair beside the bed where her husband used to sit every morning while he dressed for work. Derrick was sound asleep on his back with his arms at his sides. He had said being on his back was the best position for him to make a connection. She didn't fully understand how etheric traveling worked. He had explained that there were seven planes of existence, that we live in the physical plane and we can travel to the astral plane. In between, is the etheric plane.

Victory had stopped him, not wanting to know more. She was still trying to digest what she had witnessed earlier. Derrick could move objects with his mind. He seemed proud of the fact that he killed people for a living. He might not be a serial killer like she had first thought but he was just as bad. He was too arrogant for his own good. It was difficult to believe he had paranormal powers that defied logic and probably science. Victory would never have believed it if she hadn't seen it with her own eyes. The whole situation was unreal, unbelievable. Could Derrick find Jade? What if he couldn't? What if she had made the wrong decision? She tried not to think about it and watched Derrick's chest rise and fall.

Victory searched his face. His features were relaxed. He looked kind. Not the same man who'd killed dozens of people and assured her he could kill her if she told anyone about him or the Elara Project. Jade's life was on the line and Victory kept wondering if she was wasting valuable time.

Derrick's eyelids twitched. His body rolled gently back and forth as if he was rocking. His breathing became louder.

She didn't move. He had told her she needed to stay quiet, so nothing interrupted him while he did his thing. Had he connected with Elder?

Victory sat ram-rod straight and tapped her foot silently on the carpet. The muscles in his arms and legs tensed and then released. Sweat glimmered on his forehead in the moonlight filtering through the blinds.

Suddenly, Derrick's eyes popped open. He stared at the ceiling.

She leaned forward and grabbed his arm. "Did you find them?"

He sat up slowly. "Elder's asleep in his car, inside a building. He woke up seconds after I connected with him. That's never happened before. It was like he sensed my presence."

Victory was quickly losing hope that she'd see Jade again. "Did you see anything else? Did you see Jade?"

He shook his head and put his hand on hers. "I'm sorry."

She slid off the chair to her knees. She'd beg if she had to, anything to find her daughter. "You have to try again."

"I can't. It drains my energy. I need to rest for a bit first."

"How long?"

"At least an hour."

Her eyes snapped to the clock on the nightstand. Ten-forty-five. They didn't have an hour. The numbers stared back, reminding her every minute that passed meant the difference between life and death. Tears gathered. Victory held them back. She swallowed hard. "He always kills between midnight and three. Jade doesn't have much time. Please."

He rubbed the back of his neck and looked at her.

His eyes illuminated bluer than usual, almost as if they were supercharged. They looked different. Weird. Creepy.

"Does he have to be asleep for you to find him?"

"No. It's more difficult." He rubbed his forehead. "I need a couple of Aspirins or something for this monster headache and more whiskey."

While Derrick rested, Victory poured another drink for him in the kitchen and quickly checked her phone. There was no news from Ryan or Sean. She rushed into the bathroom, opened the medicine cabinet, and grabbed a bottle of headache medication. As she headed back to the bedroom, sickness rose in her stomach. Derrick *was*

Jade's only hope.

* * *

Derrick popped two pills in his mouth and downed the glass of whiskey, then laid back in the bed. He knew they didn't have much time. It concerned him that Elder had woken up. His presence usually went undetected. It made him wonder if the killer was sensitive to paranormal events. He had to keep trying even though he knew his energy would be depleted and he'd be too weak to try again for hours. Then it might be too late. He had to make it work. He needed to kill Jeremy Elder. It was Jade's only chance.

Derrick closed his eyes and took in repeated deep breaths, visualizing the killer and his vehicle. As his body relaxed, he controlled his breathing until he fell asleep. Minutes later, he felt himself lift, exiting the physical plane. His astral body floated, hovering above his abandoned body. A powerful force sent him spinning and twisting. Vaporous luminosity burst into a long trail of effervescing light, and then he was in a dark tunnel.

He flew with ease at the speed of light. The peaceful sound of rushing water mixed with tormented cries. Echoing trumpets blared like something from a sci-fi movie. A sharp sense of reality and familiarity hit him as he rushed by, and through, other travelers. Derrick sensed that most were friendly, others quite sinister. He knew to stay away from the sinister ones because a dark entity could attach its self to him. He didn't need to be bringing back a malicious entity. The smell of something sweet invaded his senses. *Baby oil.* He traveled through a brick wall.

He was inside a building, the same structure he'd visited earlier. Diffused light poured out from a fixture suspended from the ceiling. He slowed his speed. He spotted the blurry and wavy outline of a woman inside a metal pen. *Jade.* He couldn't tell if she was alive or not. Derrick kept moving, taking in all he could. The outline of Elder's vehicle came into view, parked in front of loading bay door. Above the door, hung a worn blue, white, and red oval-shaped sign. He moved closer to read it. *Lornestown Assembly.* Then he was suddenly being pulled back, like an impregnable magnet, tugging him backward at warp speed. He spiraled into inky blackness.

Derrick's astral body melded with his physical body with a loud bang in his head and bucked him back into the bed with such force, the bed jolted. His arms and legs tingled and vibrated as if the adrenaline had been sucked from them. Sweat poured down the sides of his face. The muscles in his legs flinched in a weird rhythm, a symptom he hadn't experienced before. Dinging and thumping exploded in his head. Then came the pain. He put his hands over his ears. A hand touched his shoulder.

"Derrick?"

He opened his eyes to Victory's voice. His headache intensified, drumming behind his eyes, cutting deep into his forehead from temple to temple. The energy drained from his body. He forced himself to turn his head. Victory was staring at him as if he was crazy.

"Did you find Jade?"

Her voice was electrified with concern, and loud. He couldn't answer. His skin felt hot as if he was running a high fever.

She shook his arm. "Did you find Jade? Is she alive?"

He choked out the words as weakness took over.

"Lornestown...Assembly."

*   *   *

Victory squinted through the windshield of Derrick's SUV. He had convinced her to take his vehicle instead of her car. She was glad she had. Headlights bounced and stabbed through the driving snow. The wind howled like an invisible monster hidden in the shadows, blowing a wall of white across the road. Drivers were being advised to stay off the streets. Most of the local cops and state troopers were busy dealing with hundreds of traffic accidents all over the city.

Ahead, emergency vehicles' flashing lights were scarcely visible through the blinding snow. Another accident. Another roadblock. She eased her foot down on the brake and came to a stop. She wheeled the SUV around, drove in the opposite direction, and then turned right at the intersection, praying the street wasn't closed due to another accident. The deteriorating weather made it difficult to drive anywhere quickly enough. Even though her nerves were shot, adrenaline burned through her, keeping her focused.

She had to get to Jade in time.

Victory glanced at Derrick, then back to the road. He looked exhausted and weak. "You didn't have to come with me."

"I had to. You're driving my vehicle."

She knew by the tone of his voice he was trying to keep things light even though the situation was deathly serious. "What else did you see inside the building?"

Derrick looked out the side window. She could sense he wasn't telling her everything. "I need to know."

"He's keeping Jade in a pen. Some sort of a large metal cage."

Victory was terrified for her daughter and afraid to ask again. "Was she alive?"

"I couldn't tell. Not everything I see is in focus. Things can sometimes be blurry and out of shape." He looked at her. "I was going to kill him but something or someone pulled me back."

Victory wished he'd killed the man. "Someone or something?"

"Maybe another traveler. I don't know. I've never experienced such a powerful force before."

Victory continued to make small talk to save her sanity. The thought of losing Jade shredded her heart piece by piece.

Before they'd left the apartment, she'd searched through numerous databases looking for Lornestown Assembly. She had learned the mid-sized automotive parts assembly warehouse was located on Bathgate Street. The business had closed ten years ago and was rented to Jeremy Elder.

"He planned everything right down to renting the warehouse to take his victims to torture and kill them." The echo of her own words turned the blood in her veins to ice. Her stomach lurched. She needed to change the subject before she threw up for the third time in days. "Can you bring back things with you when you travel?"

Derrick turned his head and looked at her. "Small items, like coins. It requires a lot of energy and concentration."

None of her questions about etheric traveling mattered at the moment. Her focus was getting to her daughter. Nothing else mattered. "Does your father have paranormal abilities, too?"

"He does. He hasn't used them in a long time. So did my grandfather. He worked for the CIA and was part of the original Elara Project."

Anger welled in Victory's chest. "They both killed?" She said it more as a statement than as a question on purpose.

His eyes flashed. His voice remained calm. "I know you'll never understand. Let's leave it at that."

Victory couldn't leave it. Did he forget she was an FBI agent? He had threatened to kill her if she crossed him. That didn't sit well even if he had used his strange paranormal skill to help find Jade. "How can you not feel any remorse or guilt for what you have done over the past twenty years?"

She felt his gaze bore into her.

"Who says I don't feel anything? I'm not a monster, Victory. I was doing my job just like you do yours. You took an oath to serve our country and so did I."

He was right. She didn't understand. Never would. Her gaze moved to the clock on the dash. Her pulse sped up. It was eleven-thirty.

Her phone rang. Victory dug it out of her pocket and passed it to Derrick. "Put it on speaker for me, please."

Derrick took the phone.

"Vic?"

Victory gripped the steering wheel tighter. "Ryan. Are you and Sean at the warehouse?"

"No. We're stuck behind a four-car pileup on Lincoln Avenue. Both lanes are closed. We aren't going anywhere in a hurry. Curtis sent you backup. They'll be there soon. He said not to go into the warehouse until they arrive. It's too dangerous.

Victory wasn't waiting. She couldn't. Ryan would do the same if it were his child.

"Backup better hurry." Her eyes drifted to the clock and then to the GPS. "I'm less than a mile out."

"Promise you'll wait."

"I have to go, Ryan."

"Vic..."

Victory reached and took the phone out of Derrick's hand, ending the call. She dropped the phone in her lap at the same time the vehicle ahead of them slid off the road, jumped the curb, and came to a stop in front of a gas station.

"He does make a good point," Derrick said.

Victory checked the rear-view mirror. She didn't need or want Derrick's opinion. "Not this time."

The closer they got to the warehouse, the faster and harder her heart pounded. She needed to prepare herself for the worst. The thought made her pulse speed up. Victory took in small gulps of air, letting them out, trying to calm her pulse.

Minutes ticked by like hours.

Victory's eyes darted to the clock.

Eleven-fifty.

She slowed the SUV and flicked on the turning signal. A sick dread settled in the pit of her stomach and wouldn't let go. The rear of the vehicle fishtailed around the corner onto Bathgate Street. "I pray you're right."

The industrial area came into view. The clutter of buildings in various shapes and sizes helped to block the driving snow. Normally, she would do a drive-by first, check out the area, look for multiple entry points. There wasn't time. Victory threw the vehicle into park and shut off the ignition in front of the warehouse.

The only light came from two large open windows near the roof of the brick structure. She spotted the shiny glint of a padlock on a door next to a battered gray loading bay door. She jumped out of the SUV and shielded her face from the biting snow with her shoulder as she peeled off her coat and tossed it inside the vehicle.

Her ponytail whipped at her face. "Stay here and wait for backup."

"No way. I'm going with you." Derrick opened the door and climbed out. "My abilities will come in handy."

She didn't have time to argue with the man and didn't need anyone else to look after, either. "Fine. Stay close."

Victory opened the door to the back seat and pulled out her black canvas duffel bag. She opened it and hastily put on the bulletproof vest. She checked her weapon then pulled out the bolt cutters and flashlight from the duffel bag. Victory wished Ryan was here with the shotguns. Her Glock would have to do. Her heart thumped. She shoved an extra magazine into the back pocket of her cargo pants.

"Do you always carry those around?" Derrick asked, eyeing the bolt cutters.

She handed him the cutters. "I do when I need to break into a warehouse and kill a serial killer."

CHAPTER FIFTEEN

Victory's hand shook noticeably. Light from the flashlight bounced erratically against the door. She was terrified of what she might discover inside the warehouse. While Derrick cut the heavy lock secured at the top of the door, she said a silent prayer.

God couldn't possibly destroy her twice. Jade had to be alive.

The lock fell silently into the snow built up against the door and disappeared. She shut off the flashlight. Going in blind with no backup wasn't helping matters.

As she spoke, breath frosted in front of her like steam, her voice a little louder than a whisper. "Once we're in, stay behind me. Elder might have weapons."

Victory wouldn't put anything past the killer. He could have an arsenal of guns and booby traps inside for all she knew. She wasn't sure why she was worried about Derrick. Maybe because he still seemed weak from etheric traveling. It had taken a lot out of him. She knew he could look after himself. He'd shown that during his magic gun show.

Derrick set the tool on the ground. "Be careful."

A rush of adrenaline blasted through her. Victory placed her hand on the doorknob and forced back the escalating fear clawing deep within her. She turned the knob. With her gun raised and the flashlight on, she eased open the door with her foot and they slipped inside.

She kept the Glock trained in front of her along with the flashlight, not sure what to expect. Cavern-like walls surrounded her, spilling into a dark constricted corridor. At the end, dim yellowy-orange light radiated a strange glimmer. A chill ran through her and her heart raced. Victory glanced over her shoulder at Derrick and nodded in the direction of the light.

As they stalked closer to the light, the heels of Victory's boots tapped lightly on the concrete floor. She ignored the queasiness stirring in her stomach and kept moving.

She turned and spoke in a quiet voice. "You hear that?"

"What is it?"

"Sounds like some sort of engine." Then she noticed the faint smell of gasoline.

"It's a generator," Derrick said. "He must be using it to light the warehouse."

A gas generator. That explained the open windows. He needed fresh air for ventilation, otherwise, he'd end up with carbon monoxide poisoning. As they neared the light, Victory's breathing turned shallow and quick. A wave of fear ripped through her. She shut off the flashlight and put it in her pocket then two-handed her Glock.

Elongated shadows from long-forgotten wooden shelves ran high up the walls and swam across the dusty floor like ghostly figures. They rounded the corner of the first row of shelves.

Derrick pointed through the opening in one of them. "That's the cage. That's where I saw Jade. It's empty now."

She followed Derrick's gaze to the opposite side of the warehouse, about a hundred meters away. The sight of the metal bars of the rectangular cage sent her stomach into a nosedive. Her pulse banged in her ears. Where was Jade?

Victory half-crouched past the second row of shelves. She observed a flood of light coming from the other side of the wall next to the cage. Then she smelled it: the undeniable stench of burnt flesh. Her heart stopped.

She took off running.

"Wait." Derrick raced after her. "Shit."

She zig-zagged by the last row of shelves and sprinted to the cage with her gun raised, aimed, ready to kill. She heard the roar of the gas generator. It was so loud, Victory didn't hear Derrick come up behind her. She flattened her back against the wall, steeling herself for the worst-case scenario, and looked around the corner. She gasped in horror.

Jade was secured in a chair. Her head hung down. Four industrial-sized heaters on wheels were positioned around her. The heaters were on, their fiery red glow burning her.

She wasn't moving.

Victory suddenly couldn't breathe. It felt as if hands were around her neck strangling her. The horror of what she was witnessing paralyzed her for a split-second. She felt Derrick's hand on her forearm.

She needed to save Jade.

Victory ran, her boots thudding against the floor. Her eyes darted back and forth, sweeping the area with her gun for the killer. Derrick zoomed by her with incredible speed. He stopped at the generator and cut the power. The ceiling light went out. The heaters shut down, their raging glow, vanishing into the spooky darkness.

Victory jerked the flashlight out of her pocket and clicked it on. She moved the beam of light in Jade's direction. "Jade. I'm here." An overwhelming feeling of doom and realization took over.

Jade tried to raise her chin, her head shaking, and made a squeaky sound.

She was alive.

Victory dropped to her knees in front of her daughter. The smell of baby oil and burnt flesh invaded her senses. "Don't try to talk."

Derrick was already on his phone calling 9-1-1.

She knew if the ambulance didn't get here quickly, Jade's throat could close from the swelling due to the severe burns. She set the flashlight on the floor and kept a firm grip on her gun.

Victory gently stroked a small bare spot on her daughter's shoulder that wasn't burnt. "It's going to be okay. I love you."

Victory's heart shattered at what Elder had done to her child. She wanted to look away from the gory sight, but this was her daughter, her baby, disfigured, covered in burns, her skin still smoldering in spots. The revolting stench, a mix of burnt flesh, hair, baby oil, and bodily fluids was overwhelming.

"The ambulance is on its way. What can I do to help?" Derrick said softly.

Victory looked up at him and didn't realize she was crying. "Wheel those heaters away from us and get the light back on. Then find Elder. He's still here." She looked around and raised her voice." I know you're here, you bastard. Come out and I won't have to put a bullet in your head!"

Derrick began moving the heaters away from her and Jade.

Victory heard squeaking, hissing, and chatter. She grabbed the flashlight. Rats scrambled across the floor and shrunk into the shadows, their eyes flashing as they whizzed by.

Jade moaned. Tears glistened in the corners of her eyes.

Victory gently caressed her shoulder, trying to soothe her. "It's okay, baby. We're going to get you to the hospital."

The reality of the situation bore down on Victory, unrelenting, vile, and unfair. Her heart clenched. Jade was clinging to life.

❊　❊　❊

Jeremy crouched behind the end of the second row of shelves and watched. The FBI agent had found him. Anger boiled inside him. He needed to get to his car, but it was parked on the other side of the warehouse a few hundred feet on the far side of the generator by the loading bay door.

It would be risky.

He'd have to make a run for it in the dark. It was the only chance he had of getting away.

❊　❊　❊

The light flicked on.

Victory glanced at Derrick. He was standing still like a statue, staring across the warehouse. "What's wrong?"

He didn't answer. Her eyes darted past him.

Elder was running toward his car.

Victory jumped to her feet. Her hands shook. She fired.

The shot missed him and drilled into a shelf with a hollow thud. Wood cracked and splintered. Suddenly, a long pipe spiraled through the air like a boomerang and struck the killer on the side of the head. He went down hard and stayed down.

Victory thought she was seeing things until she realized that Derrick had used psychokinesis to move the pipe. Her attention immediately snapped back to Jade.

She squatted in front of her daughter. "We're going to get you out of here." Victory inspected the wire cable wrapped around Jade's body securing her to the metal chair. The cable was embedded into her arms at the elbows.

Jade's head bobbed to one side at Victory's voice. Her breathing became labored. She made a gurgling sound.

She doesn't have much time.

Panic burst hot and heavy in Victory's chest. She sucked in a deep breath and exhaled. She had to stay calm.

As if reading her mind, Derrick said, "I'll get the bolt cutters." He staggered and then ran in the direction of the warehouse door.

She could tell by his speed and by the way he was moving, he had little energy left after using his paranormal ability to wallop Elder with the pipe. At one point she thought he'd trip and fall. "Call 9-1-1 again!" Victory touched Jade's shoulder. "Hang in there, baby." Her eyes shifted to Elder's body motionless on the floor.

Moments later, thumping footsteps broke the unnerving silence. She spotted Derrick running toward her with the bolt cutters. He stopped in front of her, his forehead slick with sweat. "The ambulance is two minutes out."

She wasn't sure if Jade had a minute, let alone two. *Please make it. You have to. You're all I have left.*

Victory looked at her daughter. She wasn't sure if she could hear her or not. "Baby, we need to cut the cable, so we can get you in the ambulance. It's going to hurt. I'm sorry."

The thought of hurting her daughter overwhelmed her. Her eyes misted over. She wiped her eyes with the back of her hand and forced herself to focus. She glanced up at Derrick standing beside Jade. "Cut it a few inches away from her arms. They can remove the wire at the hospital."

Derrick nodded and cut the cable in two spots, leaving a small amount of wire on either side of the section burned into Jade's skin.

Victory cringed.

Jade flinched and screamed in pain like a wounded animal with laryngitis. Her body went limp. Her head flopped forward.

"I think she's unconscious." Derrick moved to the other side and cut the wire.

Bile rose in Victory's throat and she gulped it down with effort. She clutched the gun and gently placed her finger against Jade's neck to check if she was still alive.

Relief filled her the moment she felt a pulse. It was weak. "Where the hell is the ambulance?"

Derrick dropped the bolt cutters on the floor. "It'll be here soon."

Out of the corner of her eye Victory caught a glimpse of movement. She turned her head.

Elder was standing. Their eyes met.

She pounced to her feet and charged at him, two-handing her gun.

A gunshot exploded.

The round slammed into his right thigh and knocked him sideways. Dark red blood blossomed and spread down his pant leg.

Sirens wailed.

Elder lifted his head and glared at her. He barreled at her again.

She fired another shot.

The second bullet ripped into the center of his abdomen. He doubled over and dropped to his knees.

Victory didn't care if he bled out or not. She turned and walked away, more than content leaving him there to die in agony.

She heard him laugh, a callous, cackling sound from a man who knew he was going to die.

"You're too late—your daughter is dying!"

Victory spun around and stomped back to him, the anger inside her ready to explode. She aimed the barrel of the Glock at the middle of his forehead and fired.

His head pitched forward and then smashed back onto the floor.

Victory lowered the weapon and bolted back to her daughter. She heard two male voices followed by footsteps echoing and the squeaky wheels of a stretcher. She glanced over her shoulder to see the EMTs.

Relief that the ambulance had finally arrived was short-lived. Her daughter was unconscious, in grave condition, barely alive. She saw the horror on the EMTs' faces at Jade's blackened and swollen burnt skin. One of the EMT's tried to insert an IV port but failed. The other one checked Jade's vitals then examined her throat.

Victory's heart pounded. "Is her airway compromised?"

"Not yet. But we need to get her out of here or she's not going to make it."

Derrick stood beside Victory. He slipped his arm around her shoulder as the EMT's cautiously lifted Jade off the chair. As they did, strips of flesh peeled off the back of her body and were left on the chair, a gruesome reminder of what Jeremy Elder had done.

Victory's stomach lurched. She stepped away from Derrick, fearing she would throw up. She fought the nausea down, barely, sour acid touching the back of her throat determined to keep it together.

The EMTs placed Jade onto the stretcher, covered her with sheets and blankets, and then hastily pushed the stretcher toward the warehouse door.

❋   ❋   ❋

Outside, the wind had shifted, now raging from the north. A deluge of whirling snow continued to fall and had piled up in thigh-high drifts, making it difficult to walk, let alone drive. Sirens approached from the east, their high-pitched shrieks steadily growing louder. Moments later, Victory watched Sean's vehicle pull in first, followed by Ryan's SUV, and two other FBI vehicles, housed with blue and white flashing lightbars on their roofs.

Ryan jumped out of the SUV and hurried through a snowdrift to Victory. "How is she? We caught the 9-1-1 call on the way over."

It took all of Victory's willpower not to turn into a blubbering mess. "It's bad—really bad. I don't know if she's going to..."

He let out a heavy breath and shook his head. "Christ. I can't believe this. Vic, I'm so sorry."

Victory heard the sympathy in his voice. Reality sent her another hard blow.

A few beats went by before Ryan spoke again. "Where's Elder?"

"Inside. Dead." Derrick said and nodded toward the warehouse.

Ryan gestured to Sean and the others, directing them to Elder's body.

While the EMTs loaded Jade into the back of the ambulance, snow exploded around them.

Victory's legs froze, the finality of the scene too difficult for her to deal with. Icy wind and snow pelted her FBI jacket and nipped and stung her face. One of the EMTs, the older of the two, fought to shut the back doors of the ambulance.

"We're taking her to Cincinnati Medical Center," he said, covering the side of his face with his hand from the wintry blast.

"I'll be right behind you. She's my daughter."

"Is she allergic to anything?"

She shook her head. "Do everything you can for her. Please."

"We'll do our best." He opened the driver's side door

and disappeared inside.

Bright headlights cut through the abyss of white. Red lights spun and flashed as the siren blared.

Victory grabbed Derrick's arm. "Let's go."

"I'll follow you in," Ryan said.

Victory trekked through the snow to Derrick's SUV, threw open the door, and got in.

Derrick opened the driver's door and grabbed the snow brush beside his seat. He quickly cleared the snow from the windshield then climbed into the vehicle. He rammed the keys in the ignition and turned. The engine roared to life.

Victory watched in the side mirror, her heart thrashing, waiting for the emergency vehicle to get ahead of them. It wasn't moving.

The rear of the ambulance slid sideways, its engine grunting and whining, the sound straining against the howling wind. Tires spun, trying to gain traction. The vehicle leapt forward as if possessed then stopped again.

Derrick turned on the windshield wipers. The blades flapped frantically across the window. He glanced over this shoulder. "Looks like they're stuck."

Her pulse pounded at her temples. Victory continued to watch, praying the vehicle would move soon. It slid right, then left, veering forward a few feet then stopped. Uneasiness crawled over her skin. She held her breath and felt every minute pass with anguished precision.

The engine snarled. Wheels spun with aggressive speed, burrowing into the snow, searching for the pavement below. The ambulance wasn't going anywhere.

"Damn it!" She opened her door and jumped out.

The driver was already out of the ambulance checking the back tires.

Victory met him, shivering. Snow rushed at them horizontally. Her hair was soaked and so were her cargo pants up to her thighs.

"I called for another ambulance," he said.

"It'll be too late. The weather is getting worse. It will never get here in time."

He walked to the back and opened one of the doors.

Victory followed him. She peered inside at Jade, and then to the EMT. She was afraid to ask. Her voice wavered. "How's she doing?"

He shook his head. "I've stabilized her as much as possible. Her vital signs are extremely weak. Her body temp is dropping quickly. She's unconscious but still has a gag reflex."

Victory's eyes shifted to the oxygen mask covering Jade's mouth and nose.

"She needs fluids. I can't get an IV line in because of swelling. I'll keep trying."

Her daughter was going to die if they didn't do something right now.

She closed the door and spotted Ryan just inside the warehouse door yelling at someone. Minutes later, Sean and the other four FBI agents appeared.

The EMT jumped back into the driver seat. While everyone formed a line behind the ambulance and pushed, the deeper the wheels sunk into the snow, becoming almost completely buried.

Victory pulled Derrick aside. Snow beat at her face. "You can move it using—"

"Not with all these people around. You know the deal. No one can know about me, or what I can do. I'm sorry that's not going to happen."

"Damn you." She shoved her shaky finger at his chest. "This is on you if my daughter dies."

She couldn't believe Derrick had the ability to help and refused. He could have easily used psychokinesis to help move the ambulance. Victory wanted to pull out her gun and ram it against his head and force him to help. Instead, she stomped back to the others, left to figure out another solution.

Derrick rushed up behind her. "Get her into the back of my SUV. It drives through anything."

"Let's do it. His vehicle is the closest," Ryan said as he looked at Sean.

Sean opened one of the back doors of the ambulance.

The EMT snatched his arm to stop him. "We can't do that. It's not normal protocol. We wait for another ride. That's how we do it."

"I don't give a rat's ass about protocol. Nothing about this situation is normal. I'm not having my daughter die in the back of your ambulance. We're getting her to the hospital now." She reached for her holster, pulled out her gun, and released the safety.

Ryan's eyebrows rose. "Vic, what are you doing?"

"Doing what I need to do to save Jade. We can't wait for another ambulance. There isn't time." She aimed the Glock at the EMT in the back of the ambulance. "You're coming with us. Get everything ready." She turned to the other EMT and waved the weapon to the front of the vehicle. "You. Wait inside for your ride."

The EMTs did what they were ordered to do. They weren't happy by the worried scowls on their faces. Victory couldn't care less. This was about saving a young woman's life. Her daughter. That trumped everything.

Derrick rushed to the SUV. Victory watched him open the back, then fold down the seat. While Sean and Ryan carried Jade, the EMT trucked through the snow, his arms weighted down with medical bags and equipment.

Once the EMT was inside, and the medical supplies were loaded, Victory put her hand on her daughter's arm covered with sheets and blankets. "I love you, baby." She shut the back of the SUV and silently screamed as tears ran down her face with each suffocating breath.

CHAPTER SIXTEEN

The usual five-minute drive to Cincinnati Medical Center had turned into fifteen heart-stopping tension-filled minutes. In the emergency room hallway, stretchers pushed by EMTs with incoming patients, coughing, moaning, and whimpering, wheeled past Victory. As she watched through the large glass window, doctors and nurses worked feverishly to help Jade. A doctor stitched an IV line to the inside of Jade's wrist to stop it from dislodging. When he finished, he wrapped white gauze around her wrist to keep the line in place while a nurse carefully removed the sheets and blanket that the EMT had covered Jade with to keep her warm.

Blistered, blackened, oozing puffy skin extended across most of Jade's body and limbs. Her white bra and panties were blackish-gray and burnt into her abdomen, hips, and breasts.

Victory twisted her hands together. Panic climbed in her chest. After seeing the full extent of the grisly injuries, she wondered how Jade was still alive.

A young doctor with white-blond hair and blue-rimmed glasses and a nurse dressed in eggplant-colored scrubs were busy splinting Jade's arms and legs to keep her limbs in position to prevent stiffness.

The automatic glass door swooshed open, then sucked closed. A doctor wearing green scrubs and a mask emerged in the hallway. He walked to Victory and pulled the mask down around his neck.

Her muscles tightened, and her pulse sped up. She looked at him, searching his face for any indication of possible good news. There wasn't any. "How is she?"

"We have her intubated. There is a lot of edema, which is quite common in burns like this. We have her on a ventilator due to the deep chest burns and stiffening of the tissue. We're pushing high volumes of continuous IV fluids to adjust for the shift of plasma in the interstitial tissue."

Victory looked away for a second and watched two other nurses putting layers of white sheets over Jade. The sight reminded her of Gregory preparing The Wrapper's victims for transport to the morgue.

"Why are they covering her up like that?" Her voice came out high-pitched and panicky.

"It's imperative to prevent hypothermia and evaporative heat loss. It helps increases the patient's survival rate."

All she heard was the word, 'survival', drilling the severity of the situation into her again. "Is she going to make it?"

"It's too early to tell. Sixty percent of her body is covered in second and third-degree burns. Some of the burns involve critical functional areas including her face, hands, feet, as well as over major joints. Who did this to her?"

"The Wrapper."

His brown eyes widened. "The serial killer? I'm really sorry." His gaze shifted to the FBI badge on her jacket. "I hope you caught him."

"We did." Victory paused mid-breath. "It's the only good thing that's come out of this."

The doctor's pager buzzed and vibrated. He checked the display then looked back at her. "Your daughter's condition is critical. If she survives, she's going to require significant rehabilitation. If we're able to keep her stabilized for a few more hours, we'll move her over to the burn center. There is a very high risk for infection with severe burns like this. She's being given antibiotics. Right now, our main concern is keeping her alive."

Victory looked at Jade lying on the gurney. She appeared puny, her face swollen, her cheeks and forehead charred and burnt. Once beautiful long red hair was singed at jagged angles. Large patches of hair were missing. Shards of shiny bubble wrap were melted into her skin and gleamed under the brilliant fluorescent lighting.

"I need to get back in there. If you have any questions don't hesitate to ask. I'm Dr. Gillon. Or ask one of the nurses."

"Can I go in and see her?"

"In a little while. Give us a bit more time to finish what we need to do. Then I'll have one of the nurses bring you in to sit with her. Talk to your daughter. She may be unconscious, but she can hear you. She'll be aware that you're there."

Victory nodded, unable to speak. She wanted and needed Josh here so badly. If only things could have been different. The pain was raw, biting, and shredding every ounce of her being. Jade needed her father. Victory needed them both.

After the doctor left, Ryan appeared, the stress evident on his face by the tiny lines around his mouth and the corner of his eyes.

He handed her a cup of coffee. "How is she doing?"

"The same. No better. No worse." She took the coffee unsure if she even wanted it.

"That's a good sign."

"I can't believe Elder did this to her. What if she dies, Ryan?"

He put his arm around her shoulder and watched the flurry of doctors and nurses working on Jade. "I don't have that answer, Vic. I wish I did." He took a sip of his coffee. "All we can do is wait and pray that she pulls through this."

Anger and fear rippled up inside her. All Victory could think about was Derrick. If he had told her about his paranormal skills hours earlier than he had, Jade wouldn't be...

She knew she couldn't talk to Ryan about Derrick. It was a secret she would be forced to keep for the rest of her life. Or at least as long as Derrick was alive.

"Is Derrick still here?"

Ryan removed his arm from around her shoulder. "He's in the waiting room with Curtis, Sean, Mike Andrews, Joe Mains, and a bunch of other agents from the field office. Derrick really came through, got Jade to the hospital during one of the worst snow storms I've seen in years."

Victory was surprised Derrick hadn't left yet. She figured he would have taken off after getting them to the hospital.

"I know this isn't a great time, but I have some news

about Elder. Thought you'd want to know."

He was right. This was not a good time. The last thing Victory wanted to do was talk about the man who had done this to her daughter. She peered through the window for a long moment, working hard to drive away the anger for now, for her own sake. "That's okay. I need a distraction. What is it?"

"When Mike and the team searched Elder's house, they found a wedding invitation dated ten years ago for Elder and a woman by the name of Lily Anne Sutherland."

"I thought Elder was single?"

"Me too. Nothing in his house suggested he was married. There's no marriage license on file in Ohio, even though the invitation said the marriage was to take place at St. Andrew's church in Cleveland. They filled out the marriage license application. The joyful day never happened."

"Maybe one of them got cold feet. Called it off." Victory's thoughts raced in every direction, then it struck her. "Wait. Lily called off the wedding. It fits our profile to a tee. I'm betting she has the exact same physical traits as the women Elder had killed: petite, green eyes, brunette. That explains why he hunted and killed women that looked like Lily. Revenge for axing the marriage."

"You could be right. Makes the most sense."

She took a drink of her coffee and another thought hit her. "I wonder if he killed her?"

Ryan shrugged. "We're looking into it." He downed the rest of his coffee and crumpled the paper cup in his hand. "I meant to ask you. How did you know where to find Jade? That warehouse wasn't on our list to check out."

"Excuse me."

Victory turned toward the female voice.

"You can come in now and be with your daughter," the nurse said.

"I have to go."

He nodded. "Hey. Tell Jade I love her, and she needs to get better."

"I will." Victory stopped outside the door leading to the ER and glanced over her shoulder at her partner. "Pray for her, Ryan. She needs all the help she can get."

Sparks of light crawled above the horizon and ignited the magnificent blue sky. The storm had finally moved on, leaving the ground covered with mounds of fresh snow. Perspiration dotted Derrick's forehead. He stood in the corner of the cramped waiting room, away from all the FBI agents. He wasn't feeling comfortable around so many men and women dressed in navy suits, and others wearing jackets with bold yellow FBI letters, especially after he had eliminated Shane.

After watching what Jeremy Elder had done to Jade and the fear and sadness in Victory's eyes, guilt gnawed at his gut. He should have helped Victory earlier instead of dealing with Shane. If he had, he would have found Jade before the monster had burned her. It was a decision he'd have to live with. But he had an idea, a way to help Jade. It was an illogical attempt to make himself feel better to make up for his earlier poor decision.

Derrick dug into his coat pocket and pulled out his phone. He was about to call his father when he noticed there were already two missed calls from him and three missed calls from his production manager. He hit his father's number on speed dial. After four rings, he heard his father's voice.

"Son, I was beginning to think you were ignoring my calls."

"Not at all. I've been busy. What's up?"

"President Burke sends his gratitude for looking after our problem with Shane. Did you get rid of the reporter's laptop?"

Derrick half-panicked for a moment. He had forgotten all about it. The reporter's laptop was still sitting on his desk at home with her notes about the Elara Project on it. His father didn't need to know, not now. "It's been looked after."

"Glad to hear that," his father said.

Derrick knew he was about to go out on a limb and there would be no turning back. "Remember when I was in my second year of training with the Elara Project?"

"Of course."

"There was a female recruit skilled in energy medicine and psychic surgery. I can't remember her name."

"Where is this leading, son? And why?"

He heard the concern in his father's voice. "I just need her name."

"Tamera Harris. She was working with the US Army in Afghanistan. She was uniquely different to anyone who was part of the project as far as psychic surgery was concerned. She's the real deal. Can heal anyone. You aren't planning on asking her to help someone, are you? That wouldn't be wise. It would put us at risk."

There it was. The point of no return. The guilt-laden, questioning apathy Derrick had dealt with all his life. If Tamera had the ability to remove disease and heal injuries using energetic incision, then Derrick would do what he could to make that happen. He had no choice but to tell his father about what had transpired.

"One second, Dad."

Derrick left the waiting room and walked toward the washroom at the end of the hallway. The potent odor of antiseptic and cleaning products invaded his nostrils as he eyed a male hospital worker leaving one of the washrooms with a spray bottle in his hand. Derrick walked past him, stopped, and leaned against the wall. An elderly woman in an electric wheelchair whizzed past him and stopped in front of a snack vending machine.

"An FBI agent knows about my abilities and the Elara Project."

"How'd he find out?"

"I told her—"

"A woman? For Christ sake, son. You know how important it is to keep the project protected and the president. Us too."

"The circumstances were—unusual."

"Our paranormal abilities are considered unusual. I can't think of any situation that would require you to tell the woman about the Elara Project."

"I had to help. Her daughter was kidnapped by a serial killer. Luckily, I was able to find him. Her daughter is barely hanging on. Pretty much burnt alive."

"You had better hope the agent doesn't cause us any problems. The fallout would be catastrophic. I doubt you want the president ordering you to take care of her to ensure the project isn't exposed to the public."

A doctor dressed in blue scrubs and another one in a white coat walked by him, talking and exchanging encouraging smiles.

Derrick kept his voice low. "Like I said, she's not a problem. And won't be."

"So, you want Tamera to help the daughter?"

"Dad, it's the right thing to do."

"Why is this your responsibility? People die every single day. That's the way it works. Walk away. It's the best thing for you to do. For all of us."

His father wasn't known for being overly compassionate which was what made him the best at his job as Secretary of Defense. The man had the ability to be detached, dispassionate during any situation that affected the country but lacked empathy when it came to day-to-day relationships or for those around him.

Derrick gritted his teeth and raised his voice. "Have some compassion. It'll actually make you sound human."

"This isn't about compassion, son. It's about protecting our asses. You know that."

"They're protected. You have my word."

"Are you prepared to kill the agent if you're ordered to?"

Derrick knew it wouldn't come to that. Victory was completely aware of what he could do when she was sleeping.

"Yes." He quickly changed the subject. "I had a weird experience when I was traveling. It was as if someone was trying to connect with me. It felt like someone close, someone related. Have you been traveling lately?"

"Not at all."

A nerve twanged in the back of his head. Derrick couldn't shake the feeling his father was hiding something, but he had no idea what, or why.

"Sorry, son. I've got another call coming in. Talk

later."

Derrick stared at his phone after the call abruptly ended. With a long, deep breath he dialed Evelyn's number to get Tamera's contact information. He hoped he wasn't too late to help Jade.

✳   ✳   ✳

By twelve-thirty in the afternoon, Jade had been transferred to a spacious suite in the burn center at the other end of the hospital. Victory sat next to the bed and held her daughter's hand wrapped in white gauze. Beeping, swooshing, and clicking came from the half-dozen machines monitoring and keeping her alive. Even the clock ticking in the room seemed louder than it should.

"Your father would tell you to fight, baby. I know you're doing the best you can. Keep fighting."

Jade's head and face were wrapped in bandages and white gauze. She looked like a mummy. Only swollen closed eyelids were visible.

Outside the room, Victory spotted Dr. Gillon putting on a blue hospital gown over his scrubs. Then he put on a mask and gloves.

The door slid open.

"I wanted to speak with you and give you an update." He pulled a chair over to her from the other side of the room and sat beside her.

Victory's muscles tensed. Worry worked through her. "Is something wrong?"

"At this time, Jade's condition is stable. She's still unconscious. It could be from the shock of the injuries, pain. Sometimes the body takes over to protect itself. We'll keep the breathing tube in until we're confident the swelling in her throat has gone down."

There was something in the doctor's voice that sounded worrisome. She couldn't pinpoint it, but it was there.

He stretched his legs and crossed them. "Due to the extent of your daughter's injuries, it's important to know if a patient has any wishes regarding their care. A DNR order will withhold CPR or any advanced cardiac life support to allow for a natural death."

She felt as if she was just sucker-punched. A do-not-resuscitate order was the last thing Victory wanted to think about. She couldn't. The thought hurt too much.

"I know Jade is a young woman but is this something she's ever discussed with you?"

Victory looked away and stared at the sign on the wall: *No Live Flowers or Plants Allowed.* They had discussed a DNR right after Josh had died. Jade had said she didn't want to be resuscitated if she had cancer or if she was disfigured from a horrible accident. Victory had chalked up her daughter's decision to losing her father suddenly and tragically. Jade wasn't thinking clearly at the time. How could she? She'd just lost her father, a man she loved and adored.

Victory shook her head. "She hasn't."

"Whether you choose to sign a DNR or not, we will continue treating her with antibiotics, pain medications, and any other appropriate treatments for the burns so she can hopefully improve."

She tried to rationalize the conversation in her mind. "But you just said she was stable."

"She is. Like I had mentioned earlier in the ER, there is an extremely high-risk of infection and it could affect her heart. She is receiving high doses of antibiotics and pain meds. Sometimes that isn't enough. I understand this is a very difficult and personal decision. Sometimes it helps to talk it over with other family members or close friends." His gaze traveled to Jade then back to Victory. "She's doing okay at the moment, considering the magnitude of her injuries. Her vital signs look good at this point. So far there's no sign of infection."

The doctor patted her gloved hand. "Take a break, Victory. This is a lot to take in. Go have something to eat and drink. You both have a long road ahead of you. This is just the beginning."

She wasn't leaving Jade alone. "I can't leave her. I'm all she has. Her father died a year ago." Victory saw a spark of empathy in the doctor's eyes.

"I'm sorry for your loss. She won't be alone. We have the best burn care team here. They're caring and have been through this many times. She'll have a large team of doctors around the clock, including plastic surgeons, neurologists, dermatologists, rheumatologists, specialists in internal medicine, critical care doctors, as well as a team in place to treat her mental health. It will be overwhelming for both of you at first. You won't be any good to Jade if you end up hospitalized for exhaustion. When was the last time you ate anything?"

Victory couldn't remember. She wasn't even sure what day it was. Everything up until when they had arrived at the hospital was a distant blur. "I have no clue."

"Go and get something from the cafeteria. You need to keep up your strength. Can't say it's the best food in the world, but it's better than nothing. We'll call you if anything changes." He patted her hand again then stood. "I'll have one of the nurses come and sit with her until you get back."

Victory let out a long sigh. She knew the doctor was right. She was mentally and physically exhausted, running on stress and pure adrenaline for the past six days. The thought of having to make a decision about the DNR was draining her energy and stressing her even more.

After Dr. Gillon left, she sat for a few minutes caressing Jade's hand and thinking about Josh. If he were alive, he would be devastated by what had happened to his little girl. Victory wanted to do the right thing about the DNR. Her stomach clenched, and tears welled up in her eyes. Victory wanted more than anything for Jade to stay with her as long as possible but deep down she knew the heart-wrenching truth. If it came down to it, and she prayed it wouldn't happen...she might have to let her daughter go.

* * *

After visiting the cafeteria and downing an egg salad sandwich, about the only thing that didn't look stale, Victory walked into the waiting room where Ryan and her co-workers were waiting, clutching her phone. Her boss, Joe Mains, greeted her first.

"How's Jade?"

All the agents gathered around in a circle to listen to the news.

Victory lowered her head then looked up at everyone. "Right now, she's holding her own."

"That's good news," Sean said.

Ryan gave her a small smile. "Great news, Vic."

Her boss put his hand on her shoulder. "I'm sorry this happened. We're all rooting for her to pull through. If you need anything, just ask. We're here for you. Curtis is back at the office. He sends his regards."

"Thank you, sir."

"Is there anything we can do?" Mike Andrews asked.

"Not much anyone can do at this point. It's out of our hands. Hope and pray that Jade gets through this. Thanks for being here, Mike."

"No problem. You know we've all got your back and Jade's."

Victory felt a sudden calm course through her body, comforted by the feeling of being surrounded by her FBI family. She appreciated their support. But she still had a difficult decision to make, the toughest decision of her life and it was eating her up inside.

"You want me to go for another coffee run?" Ryan asked. "That watery crap in the machine sucks."

Victory noticed Derrick standing in the corner on the other side of the vending machine, talking with a tall and slender woman in her thirties with shoulder-length dark brown hair. The woman wasn't with him hours earlier. She was dressed in two-tone green army fatigues, a green T-shirt, and black boots.

A mixture of anger and gratitude flooded her body and she wasn't sure which of the emotions was about to surface.

Derrick's eyes met hers.

She looked away and turned her attention back to Ryan. "Coffee would be good. I'm going to talk to Derrick for a minute."

Victory headed to Derrick. He met her half-way. "Thanks for getting us here in time."

"No problem. I'm happy I could help. I'm glad she's holding her own." He rubbed his forehead. "I want to talk to you about something."

The woman eyed her up and down and was making Victory uncomfortable.

"This is a friend of mine, Tamera Harris."

"It's nice to meet you. I'm sorry about your daughter."

"Thanks."

"Can we talk in the hallway, away from the others?" Derrick asked.

Victory nodded, somewhat confused.

In the hallway, Derrick and Tamera stood next to each other.

"I didn't want to talk about this in the waiting room. I asked Tamera to come because she can help Jade."

"How?" Victory glanced at the woman then back to Derrick. "Is she a doctor?"

"Not exactly. She's is a psychic surgeon."

"A what?"

Tamera smiled. "A psychic surgeon. I'm able to heal and remove diseases by using energetic incision. I've been working with the military, healing our own soldiers in the field. I can help your daughter."

Victory raised an eyebrow and glared at Derrick. "Is she for real?"

He twisted his head and glanced up and down the hallway then lowered his voice to a whisper. "Yes. She's with the Elara Project."

A new round of hope replaced the anger Victory had felt earlier. If this woman could help Jade, Victory was all in.

"We can't help her here, though," Derrick said. "I have an air ambulance ten minutes from here on standby ready to take you and Jade to Fort Meade where she can be treated out of the public eye."

Something stirred in Victory's stomach. She wasn't sure if it was a warning. She didn't know what to think. In a matter of days, she'd learned Derrick was a government assassin, The Shadow, and had been killing for decades. She'd witnessed him using his paranormal abilities, learned about a secret government project and now he'd brought a woman with him who claimed she could heal Jade using psychic surgery. Victory didn't even know what that was. It seemed too unreal. A joke.

"I know you're having a tough time believing that Tamera can help," Derrick said.

"That's an understatement."

"She can help, Victory. I give you my word."

Victory looked at Tamera and the woman gave her another soft smile. Tamera had better not be playing games. Jade's life was on the line. "If what you claim you can do is bullshit, I'll shoot you between the eyes." She knew she sounded tough and desperate because she was.

The woman gave her a nod and didn't flinch at her threat. The odd stirring in the pit of Victory's stomach disappeared.

"Fair enough," Tamera said. "I'd like to meet your daughter and get a sense of the severity of her injuries before we leave if that's okay?"

"Fine. And you're going to tell me exactly how this works. Don't leave anything out."

As they walked through the hospital's busy corridors toward the burn center, Tamera explained to Victory how she planned on helping Jade.

The woman claimed she was a gifted healer who had been blessed with the ability from an early age. She could completely heal and remove disease with her bare hands.

"I supply the patient with a massive dose of healing

energy, powerful enough to heal the outer body and heal internally any organs like the heart for example. In your daughter's case, I can heal the burns and any internal damage they have caused as well as boost her immune system to help fight off any infection. What I do is not instant healing, but she will improve over a few days compared to months or years using traditional treatments."

Victory was skeptical. It still sounded too good to be true. "Are there any risks?"

"None."

"Tamera's been healing for decades. I can vouch for her. I've seen her in action. She wouldn't be involved with the project if she was a fake," Derrick said.

Victory looked at him, wanting to believe him. He was a killer. He had lied to her. He'd threatened her. But he made a good point. The woman wouldn't be involved with the Elara Project if she wasn't for real. All the other things Derrick had told her and shown her were true. He was the one who'd gotten Jade to the hospital. She needed to believe this was the best option for her daughter. From what she had understood from Dr. Gillon, it could take months or perhaps years before Jade would be healed completely which included countless surgeries to treat the extensive burns. Would her daughter want to go through all of that if there was another option?

Nervous hope bubbled up inside her. Victory had her answer.

As they rounded the corner to Jade's suite at the end of the hallway, she heard glass doors slide open.

A nurse yelled from the doorway of Jade's room. "She has no pulse!"

Seconds later, a female voice droned loudly over the hospital's PA system. "Code blue. Room 16-B. Code blue."

Within seconds, a swarm of doctors and nurses bolted from every direction of the hallway and around the nurse's station, their feet pounding hard against the floor. Some were pushing carts with medical equipment.

Jade! No! Victory ran.

Dr. Gillon rushed into the room at the same time as she slid to a halt in the doorway. He put his arms out across the door to block her from entering.

Monitors were beeping long solid beeps and other medical alarms were going off.

Victory gasped. "What happened?"

"I don't know. Stay out here."

"No. My daughter needs me." Victory grabbed his arm and tried pushing him aside and failed. Tears rolled down her cheeks.

He nodded to the hefty male nurse beside him. "Keep her outside."

The nurse grabbed her arm and gently dragged her out of the doorway.

She violently shook his hand away. "Don't touch me."

The nurse held up his hands. "You need to stay out here, or I'll have to get security."

"That's my daughter!"

The glass doors closed.

Victory ran for the door. She felt Derrick's arms around her waist, pulling her, lifting her feet off the floor, holding her back.

"Victory. Let them do their job. It's Jade's best chance right now."

"You don't understand. I need to be with her."

"I know."

"She needs me."

"I know."

Victory wiped her eyes with her hand and watched through the doors. Her heart pounded so fast she thought for a moment she was going to pass out. A nurse applied adhesive electrode pads to Jade's chest, studied the machine, and shook her head.

"Clear!" Dr. Gillon yelled.

Everyone stopped what they were doing and stepped back. Afterward, another doctor started chest compressions then paused, giving Dr. Gillon a chance to use his stethoscope to check if there were any signs of life. They did the same procedure over and over.

One minute turned into two. Then into ten.

From the corner of her eye, Victory noticed a female teenager with long red hair, who appeared to be about sixteen-years-old. She looked a lot like Jade when she was young. The girl glanced at Victory and smiled as she walked by with Jade's favorite song, "*Sign of the Times*" by Harry Styles, blaring from her phone.

A lifetime of memories sped through Victory's mind. She knew what she needed to do.

She raised her foot behind her and kicked Derrick in the shin with her heel. The force of the hit took him by surprise. He dropped his arms and let go of her.

Victory ran inside the room. "Stop!"

Nurses glanced up at her briefly as the doctor kept doing chest compressions.

Dr. Gillon yelled again. "Someone get her out of here!"

"Let her go!" Victory dropped to her knees and looked up at him, begging. "Please. Do not resuscitate. Just let Jade go..."

✻   ✻   ✻

Derrick stood in the hallway outside of Jade's room, his heart broken for Victory. He looked at Tamera and noticed the tears in her eyes. "Thanks for coming and offering to help."

"I wish I could have saved her daughter. There just wasn't time. It wasn't meant to be."

"You did what you could. Being here means a lot to me. We tried." His gaze shifted to Victory sitting on the bed crying, holding Jade, cradling her, rocking back and forth. He wanted more than anything to comfort her. He wasn't sure how.

"I'm going to take off if that's okay. I need to go home and hug my daughter." Tamera gave him a weak smile. "I can still help Victory by taking away some of the pain using energy medicine. If she's open to it down the road, let me know. I'd be happy to assist her. She's going to need a lot of support."

"Thanks. I appreciate that. I'll let her know when the time is right."

Tamera turned and put her hand on his arm. "Take care of yourself. If you need me, just call."

He nodded, and she headed down the hallway toward the nursing station and rounded the corner to the elevators.

Derrick let out a long breath and continued to observe Victory. He couldn't imagine her pain. She'd lost her husband and now her only child. He wasn't sure how anyone could get over such huge losses.

Victory lowered Jade back onto the bed and pulled the blankets up to her chin. Then she sat on the edge of the bed looking at her daughter.

Derrick stepped in front of the glass door. It automatically opened. Nervous tension pulsed through him as he walked inside the room, his nerves tight, unsure of what he was going to say.

"Victory? Is there anything I get for you?"

She turned her head and glanced at him, then looked back at Jade. She was silent for a few minutes.

"How dare you come in here. This is your fault. You could have helped find Jade earlier and she wouldn't be…"

Her words spat out like hundreds of daggers.

"Victory, I'm sorry. You know why I couldn't. Whether you want to believe it or not, I did everything I could."

"You didn't. This is on you." She pointed her finger at him. "You killed my daughter. You and your Elara Project can go to hell."

"Victory, I know you're upset but please keep your voice down."

"Upset?" She jumped off the bed and stalked toward him. "You think I'm upset? My daughter is dead. Did you really believe your friend's special psychic surgery crap was going to save Jade? It was already too late."

He stepped closer to her, wanting even more to hold her. "Please. We can't talk about this here. We have an agreement."

"Why? Are you going to kill me too?" Tears ran down her face. "Then kill me because I have *nothing* left to lose."

Derrick grabbed her arm, pulled her to him, and wrapped his arms around her. He held her tight not wanting to let her go.

Minutes later, Victory stepped away from him. She wiped her red, swollen eyes with her hand and straightened her shoulders. "I want you to leave and never contact me again."

"You don't mean that."

"Get out. If you don't, I'll call security."

"Victory, please."

"Get out." She went to the side of the bed and picked up the phone.

He held up his hands. "Okay. I'm leaving."

"If you ever contact me again, I'll make sure you're arrested." Her eyes narrowed. "I'll put the cuffs on you myself."

Derrick walked to the doorway and stopped. He glanced over his shoulder. Victory was sitting on the bed with her back to him and her hand on Jade's arm.

It was his fault. She was right. He should have helped sooner. He'd have to deal with that decision for the rest of his life. When he exited the room he almost bumped into Ryan.

"Hey. Why is she so angry with you? What did you do?"

Derrick shook his head and walked away.

CHAPTER SEVENTEEN

Seven days had passed since Victory said good-bye to Jade, the images of the funeral still fresh in her mind as if it had happened yesterday. She'd buried her daughter next to Josh at Westport Cemetery on Monroe Avenue in Cleveland where Jade's spirit could feel her father's closeness, love, and safety. Each day since had blurred into the next. She missed her daughter every second of each day. Another piece of Victory's heart had been ripped away and never would be replaced. Except this time, she wasn't sure she was going to get through the loss. She felt numb, lost, and dead inside. Even the world around her looked and felt fuzzy.

At ten o'clock in the morning, Victory walked into Joe Mains' office and closed the door. Her boss was sitting behind his desk. Curtis was standing next to him with a file folder in his hand.

Her boss looked up at her. "Have a seat, Victory,"

She sat in one of the two chairs in front of his desk. "Thank you for putting in a good word and all your help with my transfer request, sir."

He leaned back in the chair. "Happy to help. I hope after your leave of absence you'll be able to focus on work again. You've been through a lot. You're a damn good agent, Victory. We're sorry to lose you. I hope the transfer will bring you peace and a fresh start."

Curtis opened the file folder and handed her the transfer paperwork. He smiled at her which was odd because he rarely smiled at anyone. Usually, he was too busy yelling.

She took the paperwork. "Thank you both—for everything."

"Does Slater know what's going on?" Curtis asked.

Victory shook her head. "Not yet. I'll speak with Ryan after I clear out my desk."

"He's going to be upset about the transfer," Curtis said.

"He'll get over it." Her stomach stirred. She was actually nervous to tell her partner the news. She was going to miss him too.

Joe Mains leaned forward in his chair. "Is there anything else we can do for you?"

"You've done enough, sir. I appreciate it." Victory stood and pulled out her FBI ID from the back pocket of her pants and placed it on the desk. Then she reached for her gun in her holster. After removing the magazine, Victory laid the gun on the desk.

Her boss stood and held out his hand. "Take care of yourself. If you need anything, don't hesitate to call. We'll always be here for you. We're family. We take care of our own."

"Thank you." She shook his hand and then gave Curtis a nod.

"Good luck," Curtis said.

She walked out of the office feeling like the heavy boulder that had been sitting on her chest for days had been removed. She could finally breathe.

Angie met up with her on the way to her desk with a small box in her hand.

"I'm going to miss you when you're on your leave of absence. Six months. That's a long time."

Victory smiled. "I'll miss you too."

Angie hugged her. "I'm so sorry about Jade."

"Me too." Victory inhaled a deep breath and let it out. She took the box and placed it on her desk. "Is Ryan around?"

"He's out grabbing a coffee. He'll be back in a few minutes."

"Can you let him know I need to talk to him when he gets back?"

"Sure." Angie's gaze shifted to the cardboard box. "Do you need any help?"

"I think I can handle it. There isn't much."

"If you need anything, buzz me."

"Thanks."

After Angie went back to her desk, Victory put the transfer paperwork in the bottom of the box and began to load her personal items from the desk drawers. She felt everyone's eyes on her, watching to see if she was going to break down. She wasn't. Not now. Not here. She'd already spent days locked in her apartment crying.

She glanced over her shoulder and spotted Ryan heading toward her with two extra-large coffees in his hands.

"Hey. Heard you were coming in." He handed her a coffee.

"Thanks." She took the coffee, desperately needing a

caffeine boost, and set it on the desk. "You always know what I need."

"Six months is a long time, Vic. Not sure how I'm going to make out with a new partner until you get back."

"You'll survive," Victory said, delaying the news of her departure. She finished emptying the drawers and pitched the items into the box. She stared at the photograph of her, Josh, and Jade next to the phone. Her stomach clenched. They all looked so happy. They were at one time. She put the photograph in the box. "Grab the box, will you? Walk me out."

Ryan picked up the box and put it under his arm. Victory grabbed her coffee.

As they walked down the hall to the elevator, she felt like she was dying inside again.

"Are you going to be okay? Do you need anything?"

She wasn't going to be okay. Not for a very long time.

"Yeah. I'm fine. I just need a break." She took a sip of her coffee.

The elevator dinged, and the door opened. They stepped inside and remained silent until the doors opened to the main floor.

"We found Lily Sutherland. Alive and well. She didn't have anything good to say about her former fiancé."

Jeremy Elder was the last person in the world Victory wanted to talk about, but it would help put off her news a little longer. "That's good that you found her alive. I really figured he had killed her."

They continued walking through the building bustling with FBI agents and support staff.

Ryan nodded. "She's been living in Florida. She said she changed her name after telling Elder she wasn't going through with the wedding. From what she said, he was controlling to the point of following her to work and back, and even was recording her phone calls. She was terrified of him."

"Good thing she got out when she did. If she hadn't, he would have killed her."

"For sure. Get this. Guess where she broke off the relationship? Daniel Drake Park."

"That explains why he chose to dump the victims in parks."

Ryan nodded again. "I asked her about the bubble wrap and baby oil. She said she used baby oil daily because her skin is really dry. He loved the smell of it. She also said they used to enjoy popping bubble wrap together."

Victory cringed and pushed the images of Jade from her mind. "Fun times. Two of his favorite things. Baby oil and bubble wrap. It explains a lot."

He opened the back door to the parking lot.

Sunlight beat down on her face. It felt good. Victory snatched her keys from her pocket and opened the trunk of her car.

Ryan put the box inside and closed the trunk.

She smiled at him, nervous about how he was going to react to the news. Victory leaned against the car.

"I guess this is it. No more extra coffee runs and no more catching bad guys together for a half a year."

"About that." She brushed the hair out of her eyes. "I'm not coming back, Ryan."

His eyebrows raised. "What are talking about? Sure, you are."

"No. I'm not. I'm transferring to Washington."

"Washington? No way, Vic."

"Joe Mains and Curtis signed off on it and gave me their blessing. It's a done deal."

"Vic, you can't leave. Take the leave of absence and see how you feel afterward."

"Ryan, I can't live here, be here anymore, in Cincinnati, Cleveland, or Ohio for that matter. I need to go." She fought off the tears that were ready to flow. "I've lost too much here—my family."

"You haven't lost me."

"I know, and I'm happy about that. But it's time to move on."

"What am I going to do without you here?"

"There are airplanes, you know. You can come and visit. There's only a three-hour time difference. Or you could get busy working on a transfer, Riddle Guy."

Ryan's eyes widened, and he grinned. "Now that's a great idea. What office are you going to be working at in Washington? And what the hell happened with Derrick at the hospital? What did he do? I overheard part of the conversation. You were really mad, Vic. I've never heard you so angry."

It was a good thing Ryan hadn't caught all of the conversation otherwise he'd be questioning her about the Elara Project. Victory ignored his question, unable to answer for her own good.

"I'll be the agent-in-charge of the Counterintelligence Division for the Washington field office."

"Holy crap. Congrats. You deserve it." He paused. "What about Derrick?"

She opened the car door and continued to ignore any questions about the man. She wasn't going to discuss Derrick. She still blamed him for not finding Jade in time when he could have. It was a hurt Victory would never forget.

"You're not going to tell me, are you?"

"There's nothing to tell."

"Damn, Vic, I hate to see you go."

"I'll be here for another week before I move." She gave him a hug. "Take care of Angie. You need each other." Victory walked to the other side of the vehicle and opened the door. She shielded her eyes from the sun. "We'll get together for dinner or something." She climbed into the driver seat, closed the door, and rolled down the passenger window.

Ryan bent down and poked his head inside. "Sounds good. I'll give you a call later. See how you're doing. If you need anything, call me."

Victory started the engine and looked at him. "You were right about one thing."

"What's that?"

"No matter how good we are at our job, we can't save everyone. It doesn't work that way." Victory put the car into drive. "It's time to save myself."

AUTHOR'S NOTE

I hope you enjoyed reading *Deadly Shadow*, the first book in the thrilling Assassin Chronicles series. Don't forget to leave a review! Victory and Derrick's story is only beginning. Watch for *Invisible Truth, Assassin's Prophecy* and *Vision of Fire,* coming soon.

If you enjoyed Deadly Shadow, check out the action-packed *Whitney Steel* romantic thriller series.

Visit www.kimcresswell.ca to subscribe to my newsletter and keep up-to-date on exclusive content, upcoming releases, first-to-see book covers, contests, and more!

ACKNOWLEDGEMENT

A huge thanks to Author M.K. Chester and
Paul Crowley for their continuing support.

*To my fans, readers, and reviewers
—thank you! You rock!*